JESSICA MOORE

THE
WARRIOR

BOOK ONE OF ELYON'S ARMOR

The Warrior

Book 1 of Elyon's Armor

Copyright © 2020 Jessica Moore

Edited by Julie Breihan

Cover Design by 100Covers

Formatting & Typesetting by Black Bee Media

ISBN 978-1-7358180-0-9

To my amazingly supportive family, for always believing in me, especially when I didn't believe in myself.

TABLE OF CONTENTS

Chapter One -The Beginning of the End.........................1

Chapter Two - The Palace 19

Chapter Three - Training Begins.............................33

Chapter Four - Belial.......................................47

Chapter Five - The Mission..................................51

Chapter Six - The Team 63

Chapter Seven - Encounter 77

Chapter Eight - Belial, Again...............................85

Chapter Nine - The First Battle 87

Chapter Ten - The Beast 97

Chapter Eleven - The Belt 105

Acknowledgments 113

Now it's your turn..114

And you will know the truth, and the truth will set you free.

— John 8:32 ESV

CHAPTER ONE

The Beginning of the End

LIFE CAN BE UNPREDICTABLE. When I was younger, I never thought my father would die in a war that's been going on since the creation of Mythica. I couldn't have imagined that my twin sister would die of a sickness that had been thought extinct.

Yes, life can be very unpredictable, unfair, hurtful. My mother tried to keep her faith in Elyon, the creator of Mythica and all its creatures, but I had long since broke all connections to Him. He may have created the world, but that didn't mean I had to follow Him or His ways. Everyone talked about His goodness and love, but I couldn't understand how someone who claimed to love us and to be filled with nothing but good would allow such pain and destruction to happen.

My father died in a war that had nothing to do with him. It was the age-old battle between Elyon's son, Paladin, and His arch nemesis, Belial. My father didn't ask to fight; he was forced from our home and taken from us.

Helia, my sister, left us not too long after. I had to watch as the life slowly faded from her. It had started with a cough, then there was the blood and the fevers, then the bruises. It ended with hallucinations. She would imagine our father coming home and sitting down for a meal, or she would think she was flying with me on Shilla's back when we hadn't even left the house. The light that was once constant in her eyes completely left. She was gone long before she died.

As she was dying I could feel her pain. I could feel the overwhelming sadness she felt when she still knew what was happening. She was my twin, my other half. Watching, feeling as life was taken from her almost broke me. Most days I wished it had. I didn't want to live in this world without her. If not for Shilla and my mother, I would have long since ended my pain permanently.

Some days were harder than others. There were times when I would go about my chores on the farm and get so caught up in the work that I didn't think about the blackness in my heart. Sometimes I felt free from everything, soaring above the clouds, the warmth of Shilla keeping the frigid wind from chilling me to the bone.

Other days that dark spot in my heart would grow larger and larger, to the point the pain was almost too much to bear. Whenever that happened, I would fall into a state of fogginess, curling up in the corner of my room, not knowing who came or went or how long the darkness lasted.

It hadn't been one of those days, but it was close. Almost five years since Father left for war, three since Helia had died, and two since the messenger came confirming Father's death. The grief still hung on my shoulders. The hole left in my heart never grew smaller, as others told me it would. Instead, it filled with hatred toward Elyon, stretching bigger and bigger.

I had been working out in the barn, putting in fresh hey and filling the feeds, when I could feel my mother's watchful eyes from the door. I didn't have to turn around to see the sadness they held, deep brown reflections of my own. That sadness was always there when she watched me.

"Zalan, my dear boy, why do you carry so much?"

It was the same question she asked over and over. The anger inside me began to boil. We'd had this argument a thousand times, and yet she persisted. She meant well; I knew that. So I took a deep breath and counted to ten before responding. I could feel the anger ebb slightly. I turned to answer.

"It's the weight that was placed on my shoulders. I didn't ask to carry it."

"But why won't you ask for it to be lifted? Elyon never intended for you to hold on to it."

"Then why did He take them from us? Why did He cause this hole in my heart?"

Tears sprang into her eyes. I went back to my work to keep the tears from my own eyes. I hated how easily I cried. I was seventeen years old, for Paladin's sake. A grown man shouldn't be brought to tears so easily.

"The ways of Elyon don't always appear to make sense or be fair. But He promises that if we put our trust in Him, one day we will see the good that comes out of everything."

"Mother, you know I can't put my trust in Him anymore. I trusted Him to bring Father home. I trusted Him to let Helia live. And He betrayed me."

My shoulders stiffened as I heard her feet shuffle back toward the house. She never pushed hard, but I knew the argument wasn't over. She would bring it up again. I sat on the bench on the other side of the barn, looking out over the pastures that our sheep were grazing in.

Why did You take them from me? Tears were falling down my cheeks. *Why did You have to cause so much pain? How can You call yourself a just Lord?* The blackness in my heart grew a little more.

Elyon didn't care about us. He didn't care about the pain He caused. It would have been better if He had never created life in the first place.

I had been so deep in anguished thought I hadn't heard or seen Shilla approach until she spoke, causing me to jump about two feet off my seat. "You look like you were forced to eat a swamp bug seasoned by the Brownies."

My face scrunched up with the memory of those blasted creatures tricking me into eating their so-called delicacies. It might not have been so bad if the bugs hadn't still been alive.

"You always know how to make me feel so much better, don't you?" It was meant as sarcasm, but a smile was already spreading across my face, evidence of the truth behind my words.

"Someone has to tell you as it really is." She chuckled, the sulfur her laugh caused creating a small puff cloud above us.

"Is your fire damp? You don't normally smoke from a chuckle."

Dragons often didn't smoke at all. The flame they held within didn't have the normal properties of fire.

"Are you feeling all right? Or is it just your dark soul trying to escape?"

"Dark soul?" She made a show of mock shock. Then her eyes grew slightly more serious. "I have Dragon Drought."

Dragon Drought was the common cold for Dragons. Shilla had had it once before. It caused their fires to smolder for a few days. Shilla hated not being able to use her fire. It would be days before I stopped hearing her complain.

"I do not want to talk about it at all." I doubted she meant that. "It is almost day's end and the sky is perfect tonight. I do not want to miss the best part."

I tilted my head up to the sky. I hadn't realized so much time had passed, but Shilla was right. The first sun was already creating a show. If we wanted to see all its beauty we needed to hurry. Without another word I jumped onto her back. She took a few paces out into the field so as to not damage the barn, again, and took off. After my mother threatened to sell Shilla's hide for knocking down half the barn, Shilla made sure she was always far enough away when she spread her wings.

There was no place better to watch the sunsets than on the very top of High Peak Mountain, and I was one of the very few to get that privilege. You could not climb the mountain unless you wanted to fall quickly to your death. The only way up was to fly. My best friend happened to be a Dragon, one of the few creatures that could fly that high.

Shilla and I made a tradition of watching the two suns set every night since I lost my sister. It was the one time I didn't feel completely weighed down with grief. The way the colors would blend and move together gave me a sense that there was still some small hope in the world. Shilla would say it was Elyon's design and that He purposefully made something so beautiful to give hope and light to the world. I didn't believe it. I thought Elyon created it just to spite us. I was sure Elyon was a monster pretending to be a shining light, and in reality, He was actually blinding us to the truth of His cruel ways.

Shilla didn't question my faith like my mother did, yet she would occasionally talk about Elyon. We had an unspoken agreement to let the other believe and feel what they wanted, but I knew she always hoped I would change my mind. Shilla and I had been friends ever since the beginning of time, ever since I first ran into her, quite literally, as she was trying to take one of our sheep. I had been playing "hide and find" with Helia.

I turned around to hide and found myself flat on my back. I had no idea what I had just hit. When I managed to get to my feet, Shilla had a sheep between her teeth. She hadn't quite learned that our sheep weren't for eating, that we used them for their wool. When I screamed, she spun around so quickly her tail caught me and threw me almost all the way back to the barn. Other than having the wind knocked out of me, I was fine.

Shilla flew off, but her parents eventually found out

about what had happened and came back to the farm with her. She was so embarrassed when her parents made her apologize not to only me, my parents, and my sister, but to the remaining sheep as well. I had laughed so hard that day, and eventually she did too. We've been inseparable ever since.

She was there for me when my father was drafted into the war, then when we learned of his death. She was the only one who didn't try to comfort me with false hope when my sister was sick. She never questioned me for placing all the blame and hatred on Elyon. So despite her faith in someone whom I believed a monster we remained friends.

We watched as the sky continued to change hues and the second sun began its final descent toward the horizon. Shilla would occasionally cough, causing a cloud of smog to drift in view, earning a few annoyed comments from both of us. The first moon was beginning to fight for the stage, twirling in and out of the stars. I looked over at Shilla. Her pink and purple scales reflected the sun in such a way they appeared to glow. She sat in silence; her scales still warm from the sun. I moved closer to share her warmth as the chill of night began to set in.

"Do you feel that, Zalan?" Shilla's voice held a slight note of worry.

"Hmm?" I had settled into a peaceful daze.

"Something is not right. Something is coming." I looked up at her. Her emerald-green eyes sparkled in the dying light.

"What do you mean?" I sat straight up, my skin prickling.

She looked directly at me, her eyes holding a sadness I was not used to seeing there. She coughed again. I had to rub the smoke from my eyes as she continued. "I am not exactly sure what will happen. However, Zalan, you must be strong in the coming days. You must learn to trust in Elyon, despite your current feelings. Only faith will get you through."

I turned backed to the sky, wishing I could disappear among the stars. I didn't like the way Shilla was talking. "You know better than anyone the scars I carry. I will not put my faith in someone who lets so much pain occur." I was not going to change my mind about Elyon, and Shilla knew it. I didn't know why she was trying to convince me otherwise.

"Then it will be your downfall."

My head snapped back to look at her. I felt my eyes widen in shock. Never had I heard so much anger in her voice. She always just let it go. Why was this time different?

I could feel my own anger growing fiercer. My teeth had begun to hurt from clenching them. I didn't want to say something I would later regret. "Let's go home. Now."

Shilla didn't say another word, she just let me climb on her back and we flew from the mountain. The breeze blowing past was colder than normal for that time of year. I shivered despite Shilla's warmth beneath me. I could tell by the tension of her muscles and the quick slap of her wings that she was still angry. Her response didn't make sense. Shilla had always respected my beliefs and where I was, despite her different views I couldn't understand why whatever was about to happen would make her react in such a way. A shiver, not caused by the wind, ran through me.

Once we landed, I waited a moment before sliding off Shilla's back. We had never left each other in the middle of an argument, and I wasn't sure I could handle the tension. I leaned forward, but she didn't turn her head to look at me. I slid off her back and came around to face her. By the way she kept her eyes lowered and her head bent slightly to the ground, I knew she was really upset. Yet she still lowered her head to mine. She too didn't want to part with regrets. I placed my head against the flat of hers. This was the customary apology among Dragons. Nothing more needed to be said.

She began to tremble, and I knew she would have been crying if she were able.

"Shilla," I hesitated. For the first time in my life I didn't know what to say.

When she at last opened her eyes, I startled back. They were so full of anguish and grief.

"Can you tell me what's going to happen?"

"No."

"So be it," I stated more harshly than I had intended.

"It is not because I do not wish to tell you. It is that I do not know exactly what will occur."

I tried to tame my anger before speaking, though I'm not sure how successful I was. "I understand. I'll see you tomorrow then."

She looked at me once more, the sadness in her eyes so deep I wondered if she did indeed know what was about to happen. She bowed her head in farewell before taking off with a great gust of wind, causing me to drop to my knees. She normally walked out to the field before taking flight. I felt to my core that she wanted to get away from me quickly, and the sadness that crept into the hole in my heart was too much to handle.

I stayed outside for what must have been an hour, staring out into the middle of nothing. I didn't like feeling this way. I feared being so overcome by despair that I would fall into darkness and not be able to find my way out. But it didn't matter what I was afraid of because it happened anyway. The hole I was falling into was deep and vast. The darkness was soon surrounding me. Silent tears fell from my eyes and yet I didn't feel them. I couldn't help replaying the conversation over and over, seeing the intense sadness in Shilla's eyes.

Something very bad was about to happen to me, again. I was sure Elyon really was out to destroy me. When I finally managed to come back from the deep expanse of nothingness my mind had fallen into, I trudged the last few feet up to the house. I was chilled from the night air. Mother was probably already asleep, and not wanting to wake her by going up the stairs, I pulled a blanket from the couch, then went over to the small fire in the stove and stirred it up a bit. I sat in one of the chairs, which had been built by my own hands with whatever scrap wood I had been able to find, and wrapped the hole-filled blanket closely around me.

My mind was still racing, replaying the interaction with Shilla. I couldn't stop thinking about it. Anxiety was beginning to take over. Closing my eyes, I tried to breathe deeply and fight the attack, but it was useless. The shadows that lived in the recesses of my mind had begun to take form. They grew larger and larger, their beady eyes non-blinking, staring into my very soul, until they completely engulfed me. I'm not sure how long the attack lasted, but at some point I must have fallen asleep.

I woke to Mother pulling the blanket back over me.

"Z, are you okay? You sounded like you were having another nightmare." Her voice was filled with worry.

"I'm okay." She looked at me doubtfully. "Really."

"If you're sure." The doubt was still plain on her face, but she didn't ask about it again. "Come, I've made coffee and oatmeal. The first sun has already peaked out."

It was always the same thing. Coffee and oatmeal. I sat at the table and ate the whole bowl despite having to gulp the coffee with every bite just to get the food down. We didn't have enough to be picky, and although the oatmeal never tasted good, it gave us enough energy to get the farm work done.

The conversation with Shilla from the night before still played over and over in my head, but the anxiety that had accompanied it before seemed to have gone away, at least for the time being.

It was midday and I had just finished shearing the sheep when a shout came from the house. Something was wrong. Mother's voice held fear. Running as quickly as I could I busted through the back door. I was breathing hard as I took in the room. Mother was slumped on the table, her shoulders heaving as she cried. A man was standing just within the front doorway.

His expression was grim, and he avoided making eye contact with me. Yet he held his head high as if he were a man of great dignity. I immediately didn't like him.

"What do you want?" I crossed my arms at my chest. My mother's cries pierced my heart. Shilla's warning came to me again.

"My name is Sir Gael." He spoke as if he came from a high standing. He didn't try to hide his disgust at my mother's display of emotion. "Lord Paladin has requested your services at the palace." It was only then that I realized the insignia on his jacket. There was no mistaking his station. The praying hands surrounded by words of the ancient language left no room for doubt. He was a servant of Paladin.

"So you're calling me into war?" Despite knowing that day would come, I had hoped with everything inside of me that I wouldn't have to leave. I wasn't sure if Mother could keep the farm going without my help. The thought of her losing what little we had angered me. "What if I don't agree?"

"You are to arrive at the palace immediately. You must not delay. If you do not appear in one day's time, you will be found and marked as a traitor. I would highly suggest you comply with the order."

"That's pretty harsh coming from the alleged son of the all-loving Elyon, isn't it?"

His eyes flared with anger. "You will not talk about our Lord in such a disrespectful way." I was about to tell him what I really thought of Lord Paladin and the war when he continued. "The punishment is not decided by him. Lord Paladin has left that to the commanders of the army. It is a punishment I believe most fitting."

"I'm sure you do. You never have to be on the receiving end of it."

When his nostrils flared, my own anger rose even more. "You get to stay in the safety of the palace and sit back and watch as good people like my father die."

"Zalan, that's enough." My mother's stern words halted my tongue. Despite the tears that were still falling from her eyes, they held a warning I knew better than to ignore. "Sir Gael, Zalan will be at the palace as requested."

He bowed to my mother briefly. "As for you, boy, you could learn some manners from your mother. It would be in your best interest to master holding that tongue of yours before you arrive at the palace." The entire time he spoke, he didn't once look at me. He bowed to my mother and walked out without another word. My cheeks were warmed with anger.

"They can't force me to go. I won't leave you." I turned toward my mother, my arms still crossed. She stood shakily and walked the short distance to where I stood. She grabbed my hands, pulling down my arms.

"I will not allow you to be marked as a traitor. The villagers will think you worse than the ground we walk on. I can't bear to see my son treated like that."

"But you can bear your son going off to a certain death?" The pain that flashed across her face caused all my anger to melt. "I'm sorry, Mother, that was cruel of me. I just don't understand why I must go fight in a war that has nothing to do with me."

"The war impacts the lives of all of us, in one way or another. You are going to fight so that the war may never have to reach our lands."

A memory of her telling my father the same thing came rushing in. I broke down, no more strength left in me. I crumbled in her arms. She held me there, years of hard labor on the farm giving her the strength to support me, despite being nearly twice her size.

She hummed the lullaby she used to sing to me and my sister when we were younger. The familiar tune slowly calmed my nerves.

She pulled my face down to hers. "Now you listen here. You will come home to me. You will make it back alive. I will not lose anyone else. You hear me?"

Tears began to overtake me again. I swallowed the lump in my throat. "Yes, ma'am. I promise, I will come home."

***

"Shilla!" I waited at the base of High Peak Mountain, impatient for my friend to fly down to me.

"Shilla! Hurry up!" I shouted with exasperation. She was taking far more time than normal to answer my call. "What's taking you so long?" I was sure the other Dragons who lived up there were shaking their heads at my antics, but for once I really didn't care what they thought.

I lifted up my head and was about to yell again when I saw a blur shoot from the side of the mountain. I quickly looked around for something to grab hold of, found a small tree just narrow enough for me to wrap my arms around, and prepared for the gust of wind. This time I would remain upright.

I knew the instant Shilla was about to land because my feet began to come up from underneath me. Shilla's wings were getting stronger and stronger with every passing day. She would soon become a full-fledged flyer. Any other time I would have laughed with joy and Shilla would mock me and tell me how silly I looked, but I didn't feel like laughing.

When my feet finally hit solid ground again, I turned to watch Shilla adjust her wings around her so they would not drag against the ground. I could tell she was about to make some snide remark, but then she looked at me. I could see the realization dawn in her eyes. She walked up and bowed her head to me. I placed my forehead on hers, and we remained that way as we spoke.

"You were right, as always. Things are about to change. I've been drafted into the war." All the anger I had felt toward her dissipated.

She sighed heavily, the smoke from her Dragon Drought still thick.

"When do you have to leave?" Shilla's eyes once more held that deep sadness. My heart throbbed.

"I have to be there by mid-sun tomorrow."

"That doesn't give us much time then."

Her eyes closed. It was a long moment before she opened them again.

"We should let the twins know. I will never hear the end of it if they do not get to say farewell."

"I don't know how I will tell them, but you're right. I should say goodbye to them."

Shilla turned, allowing me access to climb up onto her. There wasn't much room to get the running start I needed, but I had done this maneuver so many times it didn't matter. I backed up all the way to the side of the mountain and ran, pushing off the ground right before I would have run into her. My feet landed in just the right spot on her bent foreleg to get the extra step I needed to propel myself on to her back.

After making sure I was secure and holding on to the ridges along the base of Shilla's neck, I leaned forward and told Shilla we were all set. Extending her wings fully, barely having enough room between High Peak Mountain and the trees along the valley, which stood seventy-six feet away, with just one flap of her wings we were off, the wind causing everything below us to bend and wave. My breath hitched at the sight; even the plants were saying goodbye.

This was what I needed, more than I had realized. The sky felt more like home than the ground did. It was abnormal for a human to love flying as much I did, but there was something so freeing about it. To be higher than the clouds themselves, to feel the wind bend around us, to reach out and touch the sky, was breathtaking. It was a moment I would never get tired of.

By mid-sun tomorrow I would be leaving everything I held dear behind.

I spent most of our flight in thought of the days to come. My mother would be left to tend the farm by herself. Knowing her, she would worry every moment about me, just like she had with my father. It wasn't right that I was being forced to leave her alone. It wasn't fair that she might lose everyone she'd ever held dear. I could feel my anger rising again, which was something that happened more and more frequently lately.

Elyon, why do You keep doing this to me? Why are You always trying to tear my family apart? We haven't even recovered from the losses we've faced already, and now You want to take more away from my mother? If You really do have any love and compassion within You, please let my mother be safe. Let me come back to her.

I wasn't going to hold my breath that my pleas would be answered, but it felt better to voice them.

Shilla slowed as we neared Mermaid Lagoon. She waited with a silent question, one that I answered with a slight push of my knees against her side. It was time to tell the twins the news. The Mermaids weren't going to like it. I braced myself as Shilla began her decent, expertly landing on the small beach. Without saying anything, I slid from her back and walked to the water's edge. Staring out across the surface, watching as the suns twinkled and danced, I wondered how I was going to tell Magenta and Teal that I was going off to war.

Taking a deep breath, I bent down, my hand hovering above the water in hesitation. Finally I allowed my fingers to dip below the surface and wiggled them in a formation I was well familiar with. I watched as the water ebbed and flowed from the disturbance my hand caused, rippling in a specific patterned that would gain the attention of our friends.

It was not long before the bubbling voices popped out from the depths of the water.

"I would not want to be your sister if I had a choice in the matter. You are always so bossy, and I hate how you try to control everything I do," Magenta huffed at Teal. Of course they were fighting again.

"Me?" Teal shouted in shock. "*I* am too bossy? Was it not you who just this morning was telling me what I should do with my tail? If I had the choice, I would not be your brother!" It was all talk. Never before I had I seen two siblings love each other more. Not since my sister died.

I could sense Shilla heat up behind me. She always hated the bicker of siblings, even her own.

Shilla had expressed to me several times her desire to barbeque them, just to get them to stop fighting for once. I could hear her mumbling that same sentiment once more. I knew she was really quite fond of the twins and couldn't help the smile that crept along my face.

When the twins didn't stop arguing long enough to even see who had called them to the surface, I almost told Shilla she could have her wish. I cleared my throat loudly to get their attention. When that didn't work, Shilla let out a loud bellow. Her Dragon Drought billowed a large cloud in front of us and settled over the wide-eyed twins, causing them to sputter.

"Hey, what is all this about?" Teal shouted in between coughs. "Meg, what do you know about this?"

"Me? Why do you assume I know anything?"

"That's enough!" I exclaimed before they could continue on with their arguing.

"Oh, it's you. What a wonderful surprise." Meg's tone instantly changed from defensive to pleasantly surprised, until she noticed my downturned expression. "Teal, what did you do to Zalan this time?"

Before I had a chance to say anything further, they began hurling accusations at each other. I could feel Shilla heating up beside me.

I had to shout above them to be heard. "I need to tell you something." The tone in my voice must have gotten their attention, because for once they both grew quiet.

I took a deep breath, gathering the courage to tell them that I would be leaving, when Magenta spoke first.

"I haven't seen him this upset since the death of—"

Teal quickly shushed her. "Meg, you know we never bring that up."

The breath I had taken caught in my throat. My heart started pounding in my chest, the pain of my sister's death once more fresh in my heart. I stood there frozen. The shadows threatened to overtake me. At some point Shilla came up and curled her tail around me. She let out a smoky whisper to remind me to breathe.

When I finally came out of my daze, the twins were arguing again. I yelled at them to stop, and before either one of them could say another word, I told them what had happened with Sir Gael and the summons to the palace.

Their eyes grew even wetter as they realized that meant. We might never see each other again.

"Meg, Teal, this is my last day with all of you . . . until

I return." I tried to sound certain that I would be back, but I didn't believe it, and I could tell the others didn't either. I didn't want to see everyone sad at my leaving. I was tired of sadness, so I brought up an idea that was sure to make them smile. "What do you say we do something fun? Any ideas?"

"We have one." The twins spoke in unison, Teal's bubbly voice in harmony with Magenta's flowing one. I didn't need to ask them what their idea was; it was always the same. Mermaids lived to mess with other sea creatures, especially the Water Sprites.

We spent the rest of the afternoon chasing the Sprites around the ocean. Their watery shrieks of terror soon turned to laughter once they realized we meant them no harm. They let us chase them for hours. Sometimes they would disappear below the surface to allow the Mermaids a deeper swim. It was nearly sunsets when we called it a day.

After saying some tear-filled goodbyes to the Mermaids, Shilla and I headed for our spot at High Peak Mountain. It would be our last time watching the dance of day turning to night.

CHAPTER TWO

The Palace

I WOKE UP THE NEXT DAY with the whispered memories of laughter in my ears, the feel of the warmth of the sun still hitting my skin, and a smile on my face. When I opened my eyes and remembered what the day held, all feelings of joy disappeared. I tried to close my eyes and forget about the pain creeping inside, but it didn't work. I would be leaving. My mother would be alone trying to keep the farm going while I would be fighting to stay alive. It wasn't fair.

A soft knock on the door broke into my thoughts, and before I could even answer Mother came in.

"Oh, good. You're awake." She was smiling, but I could see the sadness etched deeply around that smile. "I've made something special for breakfast this morning. I figured it would do you good to eat something better than oatmeal for once."

"Mother, we can't afford anything else."

"I was able to save a little, for a special occasion."

"There's nothing special about this."

"Sure there is, Zalan." She came over and sat on the edge of my bed. "You will be able to fight for Mythica. Keeping those of us who can't defend ourselves safe. That is a very special occasion indeed." She didn't make eye contact with me once while she spoke. "Now, come down when you're all packed and we'll enjoy a nice meal before you go." She quietly left the room, but not before I saw the tears spilling down her face.

I slowly got out of bed and began preparing. There wasn't much for me to bring. Just a couple sets of clothes, my copy of the Text I promised Shilla I would take, even though I've not read it in years, unable to bring myself to read the lies Elyon has written. The last thing I had to pack was the picture I kept beside my bed. Holding the photograph carefully I took a moment to look at all the faces. They held so much joy, so much love. My sister was in my mother's arms, and I was in Father's, my dark hair sticking out in all directions, as it often still did. Both my parents had a look of so much pride. Helia and I had just learned how to walk that day. My parents wanted to take a picture to remember such a monumental occasion, but Helia and I refused to leave their arms, so they held us instead. I could give anything to have that day back.

I raised my hand to my cheek to wipe the tears that began to fall. I hated crying, and I had done too much of it in my lifetime. *What did I do to deserve this?* I turned from the window in anger. I stood there for a moment, wanting to scream but not wanting to upset Mother. Instead, I closed my eyes, forcing myself to breathe deeply. The anger slowly ebbed away. There was nothing else I could do. I couldn't change what was happening, and I hated myself for being so helpless.

When all my things were packed and ready to go, I headed downstairs. The smells coming from the kitchen were so good, my mouth started watering before I even tasted the food. It had been some time since we had eaten such a grand meal.

My mother was pouring the cups of coffee and smiled, truly smiled, when she saw the look of amazement on my face. The sight of everything laid out on the table made my stomach rumble. Mother laughed at the sound. "I'm glad it looks good to you."

"How on Mythica were you able to get all of this?"

"I have my ways."

I wasn't going to argue. I didn't know how my mother was able to afford such things, and I wanted to scold her for spending so much on me, but the joy on her face kept me from saying anything. The amount of food was more than I had ever seen on our table. There were eggs, sausage, and bread, even some of my favorite fruits. I grabbed one of the blue dew berries and popped it into my mouth. The sound of satisfaction as I bit down into the juicy ball made Mother laugh.

She laughed even more when I picked her up and spun her around. This would be a meal to remember. If only there weren't great sadness hiding below the surface of everything.

We feasted on the delicious food, savoring every bite. We laughed together as we shared memories of years past, staying away from the painful ones. I didn't want the moment to end, and yet it felt like we were saying goodbye forever. I only hopped that wasn't true.

Suddenly Shilla's voice came from right outside our door, we both jumped.

"Shilla! Don't frighten us so," I said after opening the door, making a show of grabbing at my heart, causing Mother to shake her heard, a hint of a smile still on her lips.

"You humans are so fragile." Shilla rolled her eyes and chuckled.

"And you Dragons are so scary," I said in mock fright. Normally we would have gone on like that for hours.

I would miss the banter and the time we spent with each other. I would miss my mother's show of disappointment at our behavior when really she was laughing with us. Shilla must have guessed at my thought because a shadow passed over her eyes. She sighed, this time causing a much smaller puff of smoke. Her Dragon Drought was slowly getting better.

"It is time, Zalan." I stared at her, not realizing it was pouring rain outside until just then. It would be a long day.

"Zalan, remember I will always be near you, if not in space then in thought. I will send word to let you know how life back here is, and I pray you have the opportunity to do the same."

I pulled back from Shilla and went to fetch my things. The meal I had just eaten threaten to make a reappearance. Mother grabbed my arm as I reached for the pack, forcing me to look at her.

"Zalan, you will come home to me, and you will do great and mighty things. I can't wait to hear about your adventures when you get back." The determination in her eyes gave me a little bit of strength.

I couldn't say another word, a lump firmly cemented in my throat. Slinging the pack around my shoulder I gave my mother one last embrace. Nothing was more painful than walking out that day. The rain even felt colder than usual as it pelted my skin.

As I climbed onto Shilla's back, she whispered, "I will continue to watch over her. I will keep her safe."

"Thank you." I couldn't keep the tears from falling. I was tired of crying, yet it seemed there was an endless supply of tears to be shed.

The lump in my throat grew impossibly larger as I turned from Shilla's back and waved one last time to my mother, who was getting smaller and smaller as we took flight. I continued to look back long after I could no longer see our farm.

I sat my jaw in determination. *I will get back home, and I will see Mother again. I promise to do everything in my power to stay alive.*

As the day went on and the clouds began to clear, allowing the sun to shine once more, anticipation and excitement began to set in. I would get to see the capital, Grand Thial. It was one of the busiest places in all of Mythica, and one of the most beautiful. I could remember only seeing it once, in a picture our history keeper kept locked away. She had pulled it out on a special occasion, just long enough for us little ones to catch a peek of what Grand Thial looked like. She had returned it quickly to the box, saying that if we wanted to see more, we would have to travel to the city ourselves one day. I was finally getting that chance.

Despite my feelings toward Elyon and Lord Paladin, I couldn't help but look forward to meeting the Lord of Mythica. It would be an encounter I would never forget, I was certain. I was determined to speak my mind to Paladin, the Son of Elyon. I was looking forward to telling him all I thought about him and his father, and for once I might get some answers.

Paladin had been king over Mythica since the first Great War, when Belial tried to gain the power of Elyon. According to the Text, Elyon had seen the hatred and jealousy growing in Belial and banished him from Highland, the realm of the spiritual, where Elyon oversees all that happens in Mythica. Belial was so furious he began taking control of the souls of those in Mythica, wreaking havoc everywhere he went. Elyon sent Paladin down to rule Mythica, the world He made for His creations, and protect it from Belial's evil forces. Paladin had won every battle since, including the one my father had fought in. However, the war still raged on. Belial was determined to take over. I wasn't so sure Belial was as evil as the Text said he was. Perhaps he hated Elyon with just cause, as I did.

I wanted to know what had really happened to my father. I wanted to learn how he died. I also wanted to find out why Elyon allowed Belial to keep fighting. If He was as powerful as He claimed, why did evil still reside in the land?

Many other questions flitted through my mind as Shilla

and I made our way to the city. As we neared our destination, Shilla turned her head back to glance at me. She must have felt my hands grow tighter around her spine spike. She gave me a questioning look, one I answered with a shake of my head. I wasn't ready. I didn't want to fight in a war. I wanted nothing more than to be back on the farm, laughing with the twins as we chased the Water Sprites around.

When we finally drew near to the city, the view took my breath away. The gold-coated buildings shimmered in the rising suns, blinding us if we looked too long. I could see the people scurrying along the ground, like ants in a hurry to get their work done, and I could almost hear the hum of conversations they held. It was far more beautiful than I remember from the picture. It was alive.

We soon discovered there was no room for Shilla to land within the city walls. We would have to land in the fields outside.

"Oh, you're a beauty!" a local out tending a field of crops remarked with true wonder in his eyes after Shilla landed. I could feel her stand proud at his remark.

"Thank you, sir. See, Zalan, there are a few humans left who know true beauty when they see it." She nudged me gently as I slid off her back.

"Oh, how humble you are," I teased back. I readjusted my bag on my shoulder as I came around to face her. "Take care of yourself, and don't let the Mermaids give you a headache with all their banter. Flame them if you need to." I tried smiling; it came out more like a grimace.

"I can handle myself; it is you who must be careful. You will no longer have me to stand next to you and make you look intimidating."

"Is that why no one ever dared picking a fight with me? I thought it was my charming personality." Placing my forehead against hers, I tried to capture the way her scales seemed to radiate heat and the smell of sulfur. "Goodbye, my friend. I'll see you again."

"Farewell, Zalan. Remember, you will always have me near if only you look within. Now go. And remember, despite your doubts and anger, look to Elyon. He will get you through the times ahead."

I wanted to correct her. Tell her it would be my own determination that would get me through, but I didn't want to leave with an argument between us.

She turned around and hovered for just a moment. "Goodbye, Zalan. I will see you again." I lifted my hand to wave, my throat too tight to say anything, and then she took off. I watched her shrink in the horizon until she was nothing but a speck.

"Well then, we bes' be off." I turned to look at the Brownie beside me. I had been so lost in thought, I hadn't realized he was there. I must have had a look of pure confusion on my face because he went on to clarify. "Where be my manners? I'm Haloway. I be your guide to the palace. You're Zalan from the Mountain Valley, yes?"

So old Sir Gael had sent someone to greet me. How kind of him.

"I am. I was not aware I would have a guide. Thank you. I was afraid I would be lost by day's end." Taking his hairy hand in mine, I greeted him in the customary way of the city "It's a pleasure to meet you."

"Likewise." He shared a crooked smile with me. Not one of his teeth seemed to be straight. This made me smile back. "Le's be on our way then. We have a long walk to the palace. Keep close to me, and don' be unaware of your surroundin's. It be Paladin's home, but there still be mischief a foot, especially with the little un's."

I had to walk quickly to keep up with him as he turned and bounded into the city without another word.

He disappeared in the crowd at times, and I would panic for a second until I caught a peek of his small stature in the quick breaking of the people. I only dared to look around me a couple of times. Once, I felt a slight tug on my bag and looked to see a small Nymph trying to reach in and take what few coins I had. Snatching the bag out of her grasp, I watched as she joined a small group of young creatures eyeing the people with intense focus. *They must be looking for easy targets,* I thought. When I chanced a look at my surroundings, I was overwhelmed by the size of the buildings that lined both sides of the cobbled road. I chose to keep my focus on Haloway for the remainder of the walk.

It was about midday when the crowd thinned out and we reached the road leading up to the palace.

I stopped in wonder, taking in the beauty of it all. "Is that really it?" I asked Haloway. The palace was far more magnificent than I ever could have imagined. "It's stunning."

Haloway was about three paces ahead of me before he realized I had stopped. "It is pretty grand, isn' it?" he said with pride.

"I've never seen anything like it before in my life."

"Don' worry, you'll get used to it," he said, grinning.

The trek to the palace seemed to take as long as the trip to Grand Thial. With each passing moment the nervousness within me grew stronger. At one point I wondered if Haloway could hear my heart beating within my chest.

"Here we be, Mr. Zalan. This be where I let you go. It were a pleasure bein' your guide today. I sure hope to meet again soon."

"Thank you for making sure I didn't get lost. I don't know if I'll ever learn my way around here."

"You'll be surprised how quickly you'll figure you're way around."

And with that he went on his way, heading back down

the path we just came from.

Here I go. Once I walk through those doors there's no turning back. I stood at the front door for quite some time. Every time I raised my hand to pull on the knocker, I hesitated. When I finally got the nerve to knock, the door opened instantaneously.

To my horror, Sir Gael was the one who answered. His eyes shadowed over. Apparently he wasn't too pleased to see me either. I stood there not saying a word, my shoulders growing ridged with tension. It was quite some time before Sir Gael spoke.

"Well, stop gawking and speak."

"There are many words to be said to you, *sir*, and a few of them my mother taught me better than to repeat," I spat out.

His jaw clenched. "I see you did not head my warning. You still have not learned to hold that tongue."

"With all due respect," I said, "you just told me to speak."

To my utter surprise he smirked, but the expression disappeared quickly.

"Come on in. Paladin will probably be waiting to meet with you." He said it with such an air of indifference it made me mad. He talked of respect but didn't respect others. I hated people like him.

Suddenly I realized how dust-covered and tired I was. I asked if I would be permitted time to clean up and rest first. Sir Gael simply laughed, looking at my worn tunic and threadbare jeans. My cheeks burned in anger. I clenched my hands together to keep myself from doing something I would get in trouble for.

This is going to be a grand old time, I thought.

Coming to a set of doors interictally designed with creatures I had never even seen before, Sir Gael lifted his hand to knock. Before he even connected with the door, a voice beckoned from beyond for us to enter.

I once again was frozen in awe. As the doors opened my attention was immediately drawn to the high ceilings, painted with creatures I've never seen before. They had wings of feathers that appeared to be much larger than Shilla's. Their faces held a resemblance to humans but they were far more beautiful and without flaw.

"Come now! Hurry it up." Sir Gael waved me along, seemingly irritated at my stunned reaction. "You might want to close your mouth while you're at it," he whispered. It was then that I noticed a small smile trying to make an appearance on his otherwise grim expression. His eyes couldn't hide his amusement either. *He might not be so rough after all, but that didn't excuse his hypocrisy.* I snapped my mouth shut and went in.

"Lord Paladin, I introduce to you Zalan of the Mountain Valleys. I believe you have been waiting for him."

Paladin stood at a small table in the center of the room, a copy of the Text laid open before him. I could tell it was written in the old tongue by the strange shapes of the words. Not many people used the old tongue anymore. It somehow didn't surprise me that the son of Elyon would be stuck in the past.

When I looked at Paladin, I was expecting him to be stoic and cold, but instead his features were soft and welcoming. A glow surrounded him when he stood still. When he moved, I wondered if I had imagined it, but then it would slowly gather around him again. He was much taller than the average human. His amber eyes were bright against his dark skin, and his face resembled the ones of the creatures painted above.

Despite my misgivings of His father, I couldn't help but stand there in awe. Here I was, meeting the son of the creator of all life.

"Yes, Sir Gael. Thank you for showing him to my study. If you would leave us for a little bit, Zalan and I have much to discuss."

Sir Gael took a low bow before turning and exiting. He didn't give me a second glance. Paladin beckoned for me to come toward him.

"Zalan, please don't feel afraid. There is nothing here to fear."

I was certain nothing in my expression could have given away that I was scared. Perhaps the rumors of him knowing everyone's emotions were true. I hated that I did indeed feel afraid. I hated even more that the sound of his voice had a calming effect. It flowed out in soothing tones. I wanted to boil over with anger and tell him how I really felt, but for once, the anger wouldn't come.

"Welcome. How about we take a walk through the gardens."

He extended his arm in the direction I assumed the gardens were. I couldn't seem to find my voice. It was stuck somewhere deep in my throat. All I could do was nod and follow him.

We walked out a side door hidden so well into the artwork that even after Paladin opened it, it was hard to believe it had really been there. It led to a white cobblestone path that weaved in and out of the most beautiful plants I had ever seen. The beauty of the palace was far greater than anything back home.

Paladin didn't speak for quite some time. At first I was trying to focus on him and wait for him to begin talking, but I found it hard to keep my mind from getting lost in thought.

"There seems to be a lot on your mind." He was looking at me with a knowing smile.

"I was just forced to leave my home to come fight in a war that I couldn't care less about." I kept my eyes on the path ahead of us.

"Are you sure that is all you are thinking about?" Again, that smile. Something about it made it hard not to tell him the truth.

How can he possibly know what is going on in my thoughts? I can't even decipher them.

"I know what Elyon allows me to know. I can see the pain of grief still there behind your eyes. You have not let go of it." He stopped walking and tilted his head as if to better hear something.

I did the same to see if I could hear it. The only sound that came was the wind rustling through the trees and bushes in the lavish garden.

We stood like that long enough for me to start to feel very awkward until finally he spoke. "That is a conversation for another day. We must first discuss about your time here. Let's sit."

He gestured to a bench not far off. Even the bench was intricately designed. This one showed an image of a man hanging from a post with words written underneath it in a language I didn't know. When I looked closer, I realized the man bore a striking resemblance to Paladin.

"Lord Paladin, I do not understand why you summoned me. I've not the strength for battle. I know nothing of fighting. Most importantly, I have no desire to be here. I hate Elyon for all the pain He has caused me, and I want nothing to do with His war." I was finally able to say some of the things I had pent up inside of me for years, but the anger I thought would be behind my words wasn't there. My argument sound flat, even to me.

He didn't rebuke me; he just sat there staring at me for a moment. His gaze should have been unsettling, but it wasn't.

"There is more to you than you yet realize. My father does not want you to be in pain. It is not He who causes it.

Elyon created you with an inner strength not found in many others. I've called you to the palace because we need that strength now."

I sprang to my feet, suddenly unable to be still. "Inner strength? What inner strength? If you were to look inside me you would find a terrified little boy crouched in the corner trying to stay alive, trying to keep from getting hurt anymore. I have no inner strength. I can't even keep myself from having an anxiety attack every time I think of—" I stopped pacing and froze.

"Zalan, I can indeed see that little boy inside of you. But he isn't cowering in a corner. He's looking out the door ready to run, grow, and heal from the past. If only he is given that chance. Elyon has given you a strength you have not quite found yet. The circumstances of your life have made you into the person you are, and that person is one of the strongest warriors I've ever had the pleasure of meeting."

"I am no warrior." I didn't know where he got off telling me that the pain and loss in my life was given to me to make me stronger. It had done nothing but crush me.

Paladin came over and placed his hand on my shoulder. Then he did something I wasn't expecting. He embraced me. I immediately felt a warmth cover me from the inside out, a peace stronger than I had ever felt before.

When he released me, I was able to breathe again. I hadn't even realized I had stopped. I looked at him with awe and amazement. In his eyes I saw so much love for me, even though I held so much resentment toward his father. Paladin still embraced me with open arms. I didn't understand it.

"Zalan, you have much to learn still, about who Elyon is and who you are, but you need not worry about finding it out on your own. You are never alone in anything you do. My father and I are always there beside you, helping you, leading you. You must remember that, even in the days to come." His eyes held a hint of sorrow, and that scared me a little. "You will stay at the palace for some time and train, then I'm placing you in a special assignment. I will explain more later. For the rest of today, please explore the palace as you like. And get some rest. You'll need it in the days to come." He looked at me one last time, again with an expression of sorrow, but only for a moment before he smiled and walked away, leaving me in the gardens trying to figure out what in Mythica had just happened.

Chapter Three

Training Begins

I was not sure how long I had walked around the palace replaying everything that had transpired with Paladin. It had all been so much to take in. The uncontrollable emotions, the look of sorrow and pain crossing over Paladin's face. It had been overwhelming. Maybe Lord Paladin wasn't as horrible as I imagined. Only time would tell of his true nature.

I was only partially able to take in the palace around me. Despite the amount of details in the design work, there was a humbleness in the simplicity of the décor. I would have thought everything would have been a lot more grand, seeing how the son of Elyon was living here. But what the palace lacked in extravagance, it made up for in size.

The halls of the palace mirrored the streets of the city outside. There were many twists and turns, and I'm not sure I would have ever been able to find my way around if not for a kind servant who showed me to my room.

When I entered, my jaw hung open, just as it had when I saw Paladin's study. My room back home was barley big enough for a bed and a small dresser. This room was almost as large as our house. The bed was so huge Shilla could have slept in it.

I quickly unpacked what little I had with me, taking particular care of putting the picture of my family under my pillow. After choosing a tunic from my pile, I found the wash tub already filled with water. It smelled vaguely of roses, which I thought was a little unnecessary considering I was just going to dirty the water. The water was still warm, and I looked forward to washing. I climbed in and sat there soaking in the water's embrace, wondering what the days ahead would hold. *I will begin training tomorrow, and I'm not sure I can even survive that.*

Not long after I finished washing up a knock sounded at my door. Standing on the other side was Sire Gael. I was growing tired of seeing this man. This time he wore a more elegant uniform, the same symbol etched in the shoulder. Without the extra fabric from his travel clothes, I was able to notice more about him. He wasn't human, like I'd first assumed. I could now see how his ears pointed on the ends, and his eyes were narrower than a human's. His frame was tall and slender, despite the muscles I was sure were well worked. He was Elven. I couldn't believe I hadn't realized that earlier. The way he spoke, drawn out in a much more elegant manner than most citizens of Grand Thial, should have been a dead giveaway. His straight back never once slouched forward, the sign of an Elf's superior attitude.

He seemed to sense my sudden understanding.

"Ah, I see you had not noticed my Elven traits earlier. I do hope that my not being human will not be a problem for you." A challenge lurked behind his eyes.

My cheeks once again began to burn as I stood as tall as I could and spoke confidently. "Of course not. It was simply an observation I had missed with our first encounters. I do hope my being *human* will not be a problem for *you*," I challenged back.

He seemed pleased by my response, to my surprise, that slight smile appearing once more. "As a follower of Elyon, I make a point of never being the cause of trouble."

"You could have fooled me."

His nostrils flared, the smile disappearing as quickly as

it had come. "I do not appreciate your continued insolence."

"I could say the same to you."

We once more stared each other down. I was shocked when he bowed his head slightly. He didn't say anything more on the matter, but that one movement was enough. He had acknowledged the truth behind my words.

I decided then that I would try to hold my tongue. I needed to have someone on my side. Even if it was someone like Sir Gael.

"Lord Paladin requested I show you to the dining hall. Why he chose me to do so, I was not sure, but I am beginning to see."

I didn't know what that was supposed to mean, and Sir Gael didn't wait for me to question. He turned and started walking down the hall.

Dinner went by in a blur. After following Sir Gael through the maze of hallways we finally ended up in the dining hall. Inside was what felt like the whole city. I soon learned several others had just arrived at the palace a few days before me. It was reassuring to see the same mixed look of amazement and fear on their faces that I felt. I wasn't the only one who was afraid to die.

It surprised me to see so many races sitting together and enjoying the meal, which was far more food than I had ever seen before. It wasn't common for races to always get along. Pixies were always playing tricks on their related cousins, the Fairies. Mountain Ogres were thought to be mean creatures who hunted for the sport of it, causing any of the woodland races to despise them. And of course, there was the age-old rivalry between the Satyrs and the Minotaurs. But here they all were sitting at the same table, holding conversations that were more than civil.

I chose not to join in. Instead, I watched those around me while I poked at the food on my plate. It didn't seem right to me to eat such extravagant food, knowing my mother wasn't able to do the same.

By day's end I was so exhausted that as soon as my head hit the pillow I was out.

"Zalan, hurry. We have to get out of here." I looked at the person yelling at me. She seemed familiar, but I couldn't quite place where I'd seen her before. "Zalan!" Her eyes had grown large. She was looking at something behind me. I turned to see what would have caused her fright, and what I saw made my heart pound. It was a shadow far darker than any normal one.

"What is it?"

"Zalan, we need to get out of here. Now." The girl began to pull at my arm, trying to get me to move. I couldn't. I was frozen in fear.

Something was moving within the shadow. It was darker than the shadow itself, and I could feel its desire to destroy me. I knew if I looked at it too long it would consume me. A voice I almost recognized told me I should stand my ground and fight. I didn't know where the voice was coming from. What it said went against every instinct in my body. A war was raging inside of me. My desire to stay alive took over, and I finally was able to move. I turned and ran, not once looking back, not even when the scream of the girl echoed around me.

I woke up sweating, the girl's scream still loud in my ears.

You're nothing but a coward.

This was a different voice. This one I was well familiar with. It was the one that always told me of my failures. It made me question why I even continued to live. I covered my ears. I didn't want to hear it. My heart continued to pound even faster. My skin was becoming clammy. The vision around my eyes blurred.

How could I have left that girl behind like that? What kind of monster was I? I knew what needed to be done, but I ran all the same. *I'm not cut out for this. Elyon, why am I here? I can't even stand and fight in my dreams.*

A thought had begun to creep inside my mind. It wasn't too late to turn back. I could ask Paladin for a pardon. If he really was the kind leader everyone spoke of, then he would let me go. I wouldn't have to be branded as a traitor. If Paladin wouldn't let me leave, I could flee and hide out somewhere until the war was over. No one would be able to find me. I would be safe.

That's it. Be the coward you know you are and run. That voice again.

No. I wasn't a coward. I wasn't.

As the first sun began to peek through the balcony window, a knock sounded at my door.

"Zalan, your training begins today," Sir Gael shouted from the other side. "It is time to get your lazy self out of bed."

"Great." Muttering underneath by breath I got up. I wasn't ready for what the day would bring. I dragged my hand over my face in frustration. When I opened my eyes, I saw a fresh set of clothes had been laid out on the chair beside my bed. I hadn't heard anyone come in that night. It was unnerving to know someone had been in my room as I slept. It was even more unnerving that the tunic was a perfect fit.

When I opened the door a few moment later, Gael was standing there with his fist in the air, as if he were about to knock once more. He lowered his hand after a moment of surprise. "It is about time you got up." He glanced at my attire. "I am glad to see you found your training tunic. It appears the seamstresses did an excellent job fitting it."

"About that, how did they know my size?"

Gael showed just a hint of a smile. "There are many things about Paladin and his people that are a mystery. Some things simply cannot be answered."

"But you're one of Paladin's people. What's so mysterious about you?" I raised my eyebrow at him. He began walking without another word. I made a vow I would learn what mysteries I could from Sir Gael. It was a mission I quite looked forward to.

How can you do that if you run away? The thought caused me to stop in my tracks. It left a feeling of sadness behind.

"What is it now?" Gael turned after realizing I was no longer beside him.

I didn't respond, just started walking again as if nothing had happened. I didn't want him to know about my inner battle and think I was a weakling.

I could feel him glance at me every few moments until we arrived at the training field. He seemed to be trying to figure me out. I attempted to relax all my facial muscles, hopefully giving away none of my thoughts or feelings.

Our arrival to the training fields was my saving grace. I was about to begin squirming under Gael's scrutiny.

The sight of the field made me stop short. About ten other creatures, several of whom I had seen the night before, were already there, all of them hard at work training. Seeing how aggressive they were fighting I didn't know how I would survive. All sorts of hurt was waiting to happen.

"Welcome to basic training." I wanted to wipe the smug look off Sir Gael's face. "Good luck, Zalan. I think you are going to need as much of it as you can get."

"You're not going to stay around to watch me fail?"

"Despite your beliefs, I have no wish for you to fail. On the contrary, I want you to succeed more than you probably do yourself."

His words didn't make any sense to me, but I saw no sign of deception. I wanted to ask him why, but he walked away before I had the chance.

I turned back to the training field and let out a huge sigh. I was probably going to die.

As soon as I entered the field, the training commander approached me. His heavy frame caused me to take a step back. I had never been that close to a Mountain Ogre before and found it very unsettling. His stone like features made me wonder if he had been carved from mountain itself.

"Ah, you must be the new meat. Although it does not look like there is much meat on you." His deep laugh sounded like boulders tumbling down the mountain side. I clenched my fists at my side, biting back the response I knew would get me into trouble.

"What is your name, recruit?" His sudden change in tone caught me off guard.

"It's Zalan . . . sir."

"Well, Zalan, let us see what you can do." He turned to a nearby Tree Nymph. "Jeg, front and center!"

I remembered seeing this Tree Nymph at dinner. He had been one of the louder people at the table, constantly trying to get those around him to laugh. Now he held no trace of humor, with his back straight and arms at his sides.

"Affirmative, Commander Briggen?"

"Jeg, I am placing you in charge of teaching this here recruit the basics." Commander Briggen's eyes narrowed. "And no messing around."

"I never buffoonery while combat rehearsing." The corners of Jeg's lip curled into a smile he was struggling to hold back.

Commander Briggen walked away mumbling something about hopeless fools.

Jeg extended a branched hand in greeting. "We wise get started, before stone-faced Briggen comes back to spawn pain."

I couldn't help but smile. Something told me Jeg and

I would get along quite nicely. Without another word we moved to a spot on the field that would offer enough space to move around.

For the next few hours, I tried to pay attention to the moves Jeg was teaching. He would make a stance and then I was supposed to copy it, but whenever he stood still, tree roots would start growing around him, obscuring his legs, which made it difficult to imitate his moves. He had to spend a lot of time adjusting my limbs into the right position.

When Jeg seemed pretty confidant I knew how to stand properly, we moved on to combat. It started off with slow movements, each of us taking a turn so I could learn the different techniques, but then without warning he came at me. With all his strength, at least I had hopped it was. I was down on the ground before I even realized I'd been hit.

I could hear laughter close by. Looking up, I saw a group had gathered around. They must have wanted a look at what the new guy was able to do. I guess they were amused to see that I couldn't even manage to stay on my feet. Anger rose inside of me, pushing back any trace of embracement.

Quickly getting to my feet and ignoring the pain from the fall, I charged Jeg. His face grew large in shock. He clearly hadn't expected me to retaliate. Using one of the moves he had taught me not moments before, I ran my wooden sword right in his gut. It was his turn to stagger to the ground. It hadn't been the same knock-out he'd given me, but it was enough.

I looked to the crowd and saw a mixture of expressions. Some appeared pleased at my reaction, others shocked, and some looked angry, despite moments ago laughing when the same thing had happened to me. *Forget them.* No point in trying to please them, yet a part of me still wanted to do so. For some reason I needed to gain their respect. I should have known better than to let my anger get the best of me.

Turning back to Jeg, I extended my hand. I was glad to see him smiling as he grabbed it. After helping him up we took our stances again and this time I managed to stay on my feet when he came at me, which earned a few cheers from the onlookers.

Jeg didn't allow me to catch him off guard again, and I quickly learned not to take his slender form for granted. He could have killed me if he wanted to. By the end of the day I had fallen more times than not, and when Sir Gael returned to bring me back to my room, I was more than relieved.

I thanked Jeg for teaching me and then followed Sir Gael back to the palace. We joked a little of my sorry state. We were slowly starting to get along, but then we both fell silent. Sir Gael seemed to be in deep thought, and I was too exhausted to care. When I got back to my room, the bath was once more filled with water. I hadn't expected to bathe two days in a row. Back home we only washed once a week at most. I guessed Paladin liked his people to smell good. Who was I to argue? Besides, the water was warm and felt soothing to my sore muscles.

The amount of pain I had endured had been more than I thought I could handle. My muscles hurt in places I didn't even know muscles existed. But I was proud of myself that I didn't run away or ask for Paladin's blessing to leave. Gael's words stuck with me. I wanted to prove to myself, and to him, that I could survive.

Still, I wondered if staying was the right choice. I wasn't sure if it was worth it, not yet.

I let my eyes drift shut.

***

Sir Gael came to escort me less and less as I began to learn my way around. He would still occasionally find me to ask if I was doing well, on Paladin's behalf, he assured me. Sometimes Sir Gael would come to take me around the city and introduce me to the shop owners and well-known citizens. I was coming to appreciate him a little more as the days went by. He seemed to genuinely care about whether I survived or not.

At night my fears would come alive again. The reoccurring nightmare with the girl's scream woke me every night, drenched in sweat. I was well accustomed to nightmares, dealing with them ever since my sister fell ill, but never had I had the same one more than once. I would lay in bed for hours, wondering why I was being tortured. Sometimes I would pull the photo from under my pillow and wish for those days. Other times I would fall into the darkness inside of myself, until the first sun would shine through the windowpanes. Although I found as the days went on I the darkness lost its strength. It was easier to pull myself out of it. I wasn't sure what had caused the change, but I was thankful.

My days consisted of going to the training field for lessons on fighting with a sword and a bow and arrow, as well as hand-to-hand combat. Every night I went to bed sore and not sure if I could endure another day, but the next morning I would wake up and do it all over again. My skills in combat were not advancing quite as quickly as some of the others, but they had improved greatly since my first day. I still had a long way to go before I would ever survive in a real battle.

Jeg and I quickly became friends and were often paired to spar with each other. After several weeks I was able to hold my own against him and a couple of the others. I soon found myself beginning to laugh with them and enjoy their company.

After our long days of training we would come back to the palace to clean up, then meet back in the dining hall and have a large meal.

Every night new recruits would come in, and as the days went on I realized I no longer wore the same look of wonder and amazement they did. I still found the palace to be stunning, but it was also becoming familiar, and I was feeling more and more at home. I wrote to Mother every chance I got, and she wrote back. The tone we used was as if I were simply away on vacation, neither one of us wanting to admit I may not make it back. I told her of all the positive things happening and kept my fears and sleepless nights from her.

Shilla and I were much more honest in our letters. She kept her promise and wrote to me. She informed me of the truth of my mother's well-being. Mother was struggling to keep the farm in working order, despite Shilla doing everything she could to help. Shilla wrote how on more than one occasion she found my mother passed out in the fields from exhaustion. It tore me apart that I could do nothing to help.

I told Shilla about my reoccurring dreams, hoping she would be able to provide answers. She couldn't. She would merely try to encourage me, telling me that Elyon was trying to show me something, and that it was He I should be asking for answers. I couldn't bring myself to talk to that monster, and even if I did, He would never respond to me.

I found myself thinking more and more about my father and sister. I felt closer to my father, knowing he walked the very same halls that I now did, trained in the same field. I often wondered what he had thought about Commander Briggen and if would have been just as intimated as I was. I was sure he would have been braver than me, not afraid of anything. I had hoped to be able to speak with Paladin, to ask him what he remembered of my father's time here. But Paladin seemed to always be in meetings, or gone to see how the soldiers on the battlefield fared.

Sometimes I would sit out in the gardens and take in

the calm the plants provided. Occasionally children were running around, playing one game or another. I often was reminded of the memories I had long since pushed away. Memories of my sister and me playing together in the fields on the farm. Shilla chasing us around, pretending to hunt us. I could still hear Helia's laughter and see her smile, even long after she could no longer rise from bed.

I felt closer to her while at the palace than I had in a long time. She would have been proud of me and happy to see me at least trying.

I was smiling at that realization when someone shoved against my arm.

"What has you all sparkling?" It was Jeg.

"I was thinking of my sister. You two would have gotten along really well. She would have loved the way you phrase things, using words like 'sparkling' instead of 'happy'"

"I cannot help the way I speech. It makes me, me. All Tree Nymphs speech this way. It is humans who speech humorously."

I laughed, causing him to do the same. "Well, shall we parry or would you rather Commander Briggen be your partner today?" I was itching to start practicing my sword skills again. I had a lot more training to do before I would be able to survive on the battlefield.

"Commander Briggen was my enemy yester. I would give anything not to have to tangle with him again. Mountain Ogres fight darkly and to the grave, even in practice. I thought for sure I was ghost." Jeg's dark bark skin almost seemed to pale in fright, and his moss hair began to stand up on end. I couldn't help but laugh.

"Aw, come on now. He's not that bad. Really, I think he's a big old softy under all that tough exterior. He's just afraid we'll catch on, so he builds himself up to be tougher than he is."

By the look on Jeg's face, I knew Commander Briggen was behind me. As I turned around, my fears were confirmed.

"Commander Briggen, I only said that to make Jeg feel better about his defeat yesterday. I meant no disrespect toward you." I gulped so loudly I was certain everyone around could hear it.

Commander Briggen was a very large man and standing close to him always made me feel small and insignificant, but standing next to him now I felt like a bug about to be squashed. I could feel my face going from fire red to whiter than a unicorn's mane.

"If I were not a follower of Elyon and under Paladin's rule, Zalan, you would be in a world of pain. Lucky for you. Instead, I will show you how much of a softy I am. You will be my opponent today. Do not worry. I will make sure you do not die, at least not right away." He smiled intensely. "Sword up!"

That was the hardest training session I had been through yet. I would never forget the amount of pain Commander Briggen put me in, and I would also never forget the lesson he taught: never badmouth him, ever.

Even though it may have been the hardest session, it was the most memorable and helpful. Several times during our practice I was able to hold my own, both to my surprise and his. It was the first fight with Commander Briggen that I was able to predict some of his strikes and block them, probably because I was intent on not embarrassing myself too badly for the second time that day. From then on Commander Briggen seemed to hold a higher respect for me, as did some of the other recruits.

"Next time would you warn me if a two-ton Mountain Ogre is right behind me before I start bad-mouthing him?" I hissed at Jeg as I limped my way back to the armory to hang up my sword.

"You should have pictured better than to speech about Commander Briggen like that."

I wanted to wipe the smug expression off his face. "I was trying to make you feel better. You should be thanking me for giving the guys a better story to talk about." I shoved his arm.

"I reckon you are right. Gratitude to you." He shoved me back.

"I need to clean up before heading up to the dinner hall. Lord Paladin might not like it if I came to dinner smelling like the bogs."

"None of us would take a shine to that. See you there."

Little did I know I would not be making it to dinner that night.

CHAPTER FOUR

Belial

"WELL DONE." The time has finally come. I, Belial, am going to get the revenge I have been planning for centuries. "Go tell our friend to get ready. We make our move tonight."

"Yes, Belial." My most trusted soldier bows, then exits quickly to carry out my order.

After so many years of trying to gain the upper hand, here is my chance. I knew placing that fool inside the palace would eventually lead to reward. So many years waiting and searching have been worth it. I can taste the sweetness of victory. My forked tongue slithers across my lips involuntarily.

"When will I get to sssink my teeth into sssomething? It hasss been far too long sssince I tasssted flesssh." Deceit's hissing grates on my nerves.

"I can't wait to sharpen my horns again. Why must we continue to hide under this blasted cloak like cowards?" Hatred's voice comes loud in my ear.

"I am not a coward." My voice bellows with all the anger that lives within me. Deceit hisses in fear. "I have told you before to watch yourself, Hatred. I will not warn you again." Hatred is not so easily frightened. It irritates me.

"Forgive my insolence, Lord. I so hate being trapped underneath this hood. Even Deceit is allowed to peek out from time to time."

"Don't drag me into thisss."

I rub my paw over my face. I hate Elyon all the more for cursing me with three heads when He banished me. It triples the headaches.

"Soon, Hatred, very soon. For now it is time we visit our guest. I am sure he is itching to learn his son is alive and well. At least for the time being."

Hatred baas with pleasure. "Thank you, my lord."

I make my way to the back of the room and slip through a door I have hidden into the wall. Paladin's spies are everywhere, even in my own fortress. I can't take any chances. Taking the dark tunnels that only we know about, I descend into the very depth of the fortress. The closer I get to the dungeons, the more my anticipation of the fun grows.

At last we approach the dungeons. I make sure my cloak is wrapped securely around me, much to the protest of those within. After checking to see that no one is on the other side, I slip through the wall. The room is pitch black. I do not like light very much and have grown accustomed to seeing in the dark. Light reminds me too much of the place I used to call home. The place I was kicked out of. And for what? All I wanted was more power. Was that too much to ask? He thought so. Running to Elyon and telling him all I was doing. Elyon didn't even question Paladin. Instead, He threw me into Mythica, this hellhole where I am forced to live with His pathetic creatures.

Over the millennium I have grown accustomed to my surroundings and have learned to use the nightmarish qualities of this place to my advantage. I quickly made this my dominion, building a fortress deep within the Valley of the Lost.

Nothing makes me smile more than the screams of those I deceive when they realize everything I ever told them was a lie, or at least not the whole truth. Everything was going great, until Elyon had to go and send down Paladin to try and stop me, again.

I am sure Elyon regrets the day He kicked me out. I have caused nothing but trouble for Him ever since.

I quickly find the cell I want and slip in undetected. I extend the claws on one of my paws and scrape them against the wall. The frightening shuffle that comes from the lump in the corner makes me grin. I live for these moments. I move to the other side and scrape my claw again. This time there is a whimper.

"What . . . what do you want?" His voice is so small, so weak. Pathetic, just like all Elyon's creatures.

"Is that any way to talk to your host?" The singsong sound of my voice almost makes me sick. "I give you food, water, and a place to sleep and that is how you repay me? And to think I was going to tell you some good news."

I watch as the man unwraps himself slightly. "What good news could you possibly have?"

"Good is all a matter of perspective. I will ignore your insolence and tell you anyway." I allow a moment of silence before I lean over him and whisper in his ear, "We found your son."

The sharp inhale of breath from the man gives me such delight. I so enjoy feeling his suffering and fear.

"Don't you dare lay a hand on him!" The man tries hard to sound intimidating. It is cute.

"Oh, I would not dare. I hope to reunite you two soon. I am sure it has been such a hardship being away from him all these years. Especially since he believes you are dead." A single tear begins to fall down his face. I can feel the anger starting to rise in him. "He probably hates you for leaving him, for not being there when your daughter died."

The yell that emanates from the man was so forceful I might have taken a step back if I was not prepared for it. It makes me thrilled every time I cause someone to feel so much hatred.

The man lunges at me, pulling at the chains nailed to the wall. He snarls and snaps like an animal. My favorite sight.

"Well, if that's how you want to play." I drop the cloak and let the others out to join the fun. The screams that ensue are glorious.

CHAPTER FIVE

The Mission

WHEN I ARRIVED AT MY CHAMBERS Maggi was knocking on my door.

"Oh, thank Elyon, there you are," said the high-energy Forest Sprite. "You are not an easy person to find. We just missed each other at the training field. I checked there first, but you had already left. Paladin has requested your presence in his study immediately. We must be on our way. Paladin said it was urgent, which is why he sent me instead of Gael. Gael can be so slow sometimes, no one is faster than me. Come on, let's go. We're wasting time standing here talking." Maggi spoke so fast I had to concentrate to understand what she was saying.

I had encountered Maggi a few times, and she never seemed to stop moving at the speed of light. Even as she spoke, she was fidgeting about. I guessed that was why she was Paladin's head messenger. No one could move as quickly and proficiently as she could.

Maggi went zooming off before I could respond. I tried to follow her as best I could, but I kept losing sight of her. It was a good thing I had explored the palace halls with what little down time I had or I would have been lost after a couple of turns.

When I finally arrived at the study, Maggi was there waiting, a bemused smile on her small face. She turned and knocked on the door without saying a word. Hearing how loud her knock was startled me. Maggi's hands were so tiny. They shouldn't have been able to make such a loud noise against the wood, yet they had. I shook my head in wonder and puzzlement for what must have been the thousandth time since arriving at the palace. The things that happened within these walls defied the laws of nature, but no one else seemed to question it.

A reply must have come from the other side that I couldn't hear because Maggi pushed the what should have been too heavy door open.

I had not been in Paladin's study since the first day I arrived at the palace. It was just as jaw-droppingly stunning the second time walking in. I had been so anxious about encountering Paladin the first time that I hadn't noticed the vast amount of volumes that covered the walls. I was able to make out some of the titles now. I didn't have to be a scholar to know this was a rare collection. I suspected many of them were original copies.

The table was covered with all sorts of maps and letters. I wondered if they were for the war, but I couldn't inspect them closer to be sure. Other creatures were in the room, and they were all looking at me. I recognized a couple of them from the training field. My hands grew sweaty. I hated being stared at, let alone by five different creatures.

"Thank you, Maggi," Paladin said. She bowed before zipping out the door so fast I didn't see her leave. I realized she had slowed way down on our walk to Paladin's office so that I would be able to follow her. I couldn't imagine trying to follow her normal speed.

"Thank you all for coming. I am sorry to send for you all in such a rush, but time is of the essence. We must move quickly if our plan is to work."

He gestured to the chairs around the table. Taking our seats, we all looked at one another. Looks of confusion and worry were mirrored on everyone's faces.

I thought Paladin was going to get right into what our mission was, but he instead spoke of history.

He told us that in the days of the first battle, nearly a hundred years ago, many lives were lost, far more than had been lost since. Belial had gained control of the Arachne, vicious giant spider creatures, and raided all Mythica. They covered everything in webs and darkness. Those who followed Elyon fought with strength and valor, but it wasn't enough. Belial gained more and more people under his command. Anyone who fought back was frozen, their souls taken from them. Elyon's people were quickly being overtaken, so He sent Paladin down to Mythica.

Paladin brought with him a set of armor. The Armor. All armor to come thereafter would be modeled after this armor, but Paladin's Armor was special. This Armor possessed the ability to make the wearer undefeatable. Infused with power straight from Elyon Himself. The Belt granted the wearer truth, the Shoes gave peace, the Shield offered impenetrable protection, the Helmet protected the mind and gave wisdom, and the Sword could pierce through anything, even darkness itself. Paladin used this armor to defeat Belial, causing him to retreat. Belial lost many of those he held command over, including the Arachne, who hadn't been seen since, but he did not give up.

Eventually the Armor was stolen by Belial. He gained control of the mind of a servant and forced him to take the Armor while Paladin slept. Elyon anticipated this, so He had instilled it with special protections. Belial had tried to use it once, but it had caused horrifying burns.

Only a true warrior of Elyon could wear the Armor, and not just any follower of Elyon, but someone He had chosen, someone with more strength than all the rest. This warrior would be the one to resist Belial, to lead the others to fight and defend themselves again Belial and his dark forces.

When Belial had discovered what Elyon had done, he hid the pieces of the Armor across Mythica and placed creatures of darkness to protect them and was now seeking this warrior to destroy him.

"That warrior is now of proper age, and he or she will learn soon of the destiny set before them. It is time to find the Armor, so when the time is right, this warrior will be able to stand up against Belial and inspire others to do the same."

I was confused. Wasn't Paladin the warrior? I looked around and could see the same question in the eyes of the others. Lord Paladin must have seen it too because he said, "I was sent here to be an example. The warrior will look at all I have done and know what he too must do. I will not be able to don the Armor myself this time, for reasons only known by my father."

The sadness in his eyes that I had seen when we spoke in the garden returned.

"Belial's forces keep growing. He has lured away many of Elyon's followers by deceiving them, manipulating them, and turning them against each other, and he continues to do so. The task I place in your hands will not be an easy one, and you may very well face death. You will need to set out and find the Armor and get it to the warrior before Belial can finish growing his army. Only when you find the first piece of the Armor will Elyon reveal to you who must wear it." His eyes brimmed with tears. "I, with Elyon's guidance, have selected each one of you carefully, and with purpose. You are to embark in eight moon's time and find the missing Armor, Elyon willing. "You will spend the next several days training and preparing. Learning each other's strengths and weaknesses. You will need to rely on each other and trust one another with your lives."

He then went around one by one and introduced everyone. Sage was a Satyr from Willow Woods. She wore the simple clothes of her people, which were made from the bark of the fallen trees of her home. She appeared human, but only from the waist up, except for the horns wrapped around the top of her head, hidden by the willowy strands of her hair. Below her long cloak were the legs of a goat.

Julio was a Centaur from the Barren Valleys, the driest land in all Mythica. Nothing but sand as far as the eye could see. Only a select few creatures could survive in those conditions. Centaurs preferred it. Centuries of living there has caused the skin of the Centaurs to gray and crack, but they didn't seem to mind.

Paladin next introduced Kitsune. I had heard many stories of this creature's mischief. The Three-Tailed Foxes might look cute and appear harmless, but they were far smarter than they let on, and they loved to use that to their advantage. They were the most conniving of the west Mythians.

It wasn't until Paladin reached the corner of the room that I noticed a fifth person. She was leaning against the wall as if she would much rather be anywhere else, yet her eyes were alert and filled with something akin to excitement. I had seen her before, though I couldn't recall where.

Paladin told us her name was Talia and that she came from the Fae Meadows. Suddenly I remembered where I had seen her before. I wished I hadn't. My palms crew sweaty, and my vision began to blur. It was getting harder to breath.

I could hear her screams.

I gripped the edge of my chair, willing myself not to allow the darkness to overcome me. I needed to keep my anxiety under control. I didn't want others to see me panic. If the others knew I dealt with attacks they would look at me as a weakling, and that was the last thing I wanted.

"Have peace, Zalan."

The attack stopped as quickly as it had come on. The screaming faded. There was another voice inside of my head. I was thankful for the calm it had over me. I was afraid that answering the voices in my head would be a sure path to insanity, but the yearning to know who had spoken overcame me.

Who are you?

"*I am the one who has always been with you, even when you have tried to push Me away. My name is Elyon.*"

Anger quickly began to boil inside of me.

How can You say You've always been with me? Where were You when my father and sister died? Where were You every time the darkness closed in on me? Why choose now to show Yourself?

"*Zalan, I have always been with you. It is you who have distanced yourself from Me. You closed off your heart so I could not speak with you.*"

I have not stopped hating You. Why can You speak to me now?

"*Paladin. My son has a way of softening hearts. He has slowly been working on yours.*"

I didn't respond. I didn't even know how to. I didn't like talking with Elyon. I didn't like how He said I was the one to have closed Him out. It wasn't true. I had tried talking with Him before, and He never responded. That was on Him.

Why do I dream of Talia, a girl I've never met before? Why do I keep leaving her behind to face the Shadow on her own? The questions came before I had time to give them permission.

"*That answer will come to you when you are ready to hear it.*"

I'm ready to hear it now. I need to know why I am here. Why I keep having that terrifying dream, and why the girl I have been leaving to die in that dream is now standing in front of me.

Now there was nothing but silence. I couldn't stand it. Elyon started talking to me, and the moment I decided to ask Him anything, He left? My face was warm with anger, and I was sure red splotches were all over my cheeks. Realizing I had been inside my head for quite some time, I glanced over at Paladin, who was now introducing me to the group.

All eyes were back on me. All heat left my face. I gulped

loudly, earning some head tilts from a couple of the others who must have heard it. Paladin himself seemed to be studying me more closely. The introduction wasn't long, and soon the heads turned back to Paladin as he went on to explain more of our mission.

I chanced a look at Talia and found she was looking back. Our eyes locked for just a second before I quickly looked away, pretending to be listening to Paladin. In the brief moment our eyes met I had almost been certain she could see straight through me, as if she knew what I was thinking and feeling. For the rest of the meeting I could feel her gaze on me. I didn't like it. I didn't like any of this. I was the one supposed to be perplexed by *her*, yet she kept watching me.

It was hard to pay attention to what Paladin was saying. So many thoughts were running through my head, and I couldn't sort them all out. I kept wondering why Elyon would want to talk with me but would not answer my questions. I also couldn't forget the feeling that had overcome me when He first spoke. It didn't make sense that the God whom I had come to hate so much would allow me to feel that kind of peace.

I was one of the first ones out the door when Paladin dismissed us. He had told us there would be warm food waiting for us in our chambers since we had missed dinner with the others. He had also encouraged us to first spend time together and get to know one other, but right then I didn't feel like socializing. I wanted nothing more than to get some air.

I needed to get away from everything, I needed to process. I rushed for the front doors, swinging them wide open, much to the surprise of the doorman.

Then I ran.

I didn't have any destination in mind, I just needed to keep moving. Before I knew it, I had run all the way to the center of the city. The town was deserted at this time of day. Everyone was home with their families, enjoying their final meal of the day or already in bed sleeping.

Sitting on the fountain wall I stared into the water. My mind was blank for the first time that day as I watched the fish swim. The moons were bright that night, showering everything in a pale blue light. The fish looked like tiny little stars swirling around in the water. They were mesmerizing.

But even they weren't enough to keep the thoughts at bay forever. *This is it. I'm going to go to Elyon knows where and get myself killed. I can't believe this is happening to me. I won't ever make it back to Mother.*

The last realization did it. I broke down right there in the center of the city. I wept until I could weep no more, then sat there, numb. I heard a sudden snap behind me. I sprang to my feet and was about to run when a voice I vaguely recognized spoke.

"It's dangerous here at night. You never know who might be lurking in the shadows."

The voice was deep and smooth. Inviting and friendly. Yet I sensed a warning in the tone that told me he couldn't be trusted.

The man who stepped out from the shadows had bright eyes and a wide smile, with very sharp teeth. He wore a hood that barely allowed his lion's face to show. The angles of his muzzle were soft and gentle. He reminded me a lot of the depictions of Elyon. "My friend, why are you out here, away from your friends in the palace?"

"I am not your friend, and how do you know I came from the palace?" He didn't seem to have any intent to harm me, but I couldn't help being suspicious of him.

"I have a friend there. He told me about you." His smile grew unnaturally wider.

"Who? Why would he have told you about me? Who am

I to you?" I knew I should run, but something made me stay.

"He saw something within you that I'm extremely interested in. You, my friend, have a power that others do not." His eyes bore into me. A hissing noise came from somewhere behind the man and then a sharp pain sprang from my ankle. The man's stare prevented me from looking down to see what had caused it. I could feel my mind grow foggy.

"You have the wrong guy. I have no special power. I am just a weakling, a coward. And I am *not* your friend." My words were beginning to slur. I couldn't clear my head.

He ignored my statement and repeated his first question. "Why are you out here alone after dark?"

With the fog growing heavier in my head, I couldn't keep myself from answering him. "I had a lot on my mind and needed to get away to clear it. I'm about to go on a very dangerous assignment . . ." That thought allowed for a little clarity to come back. I had to get out of there. "There's a lot to prepare for, and I best be getting back now."

"There's no need to hurry off. I'm not going to hurt you." His voice seemed to get even smoother. The way he said it made me feel as if he thought someone else would. "Let me walk with you, make sure you don't encounter any ruffian along the way. It would be a shame if any harm came to you."

I didn't remember agreeing to this, but I found myself walking alongside him regardless. We were heading toward the palace, and yet it felt like we weren't getting any closer to it.

"You seem to be troubled. You can tell me what it is. I would love to help you reason it out, my friend."

I didn't fight him again for calling me his friend. My mind was heavy, and I could barely think straight. The road before us move like waves, causing me to stumble. "I must sacrifice myself for a war I couldn't care less about. I'm being

forced to follow the will of a God I want nothing to do with."
Why was I telling him all this? I knew I shouldn't trust him,
yet the words kept flowing from my mouth. "My mother will
soon have no family left because I'm too weak and too much
of a coward to fight against the authorities leading me to my
death."

"Why do they not give you a choice?"

"Of course I have a choice. I could run away and be
known has a coward, or I could accept the task given to me
and most likely die along the way, because I'm a coward."

"That doesn't sound like much of a choice to me. It seems
like you are being forced into being something you clearly
are not. Doomed if you do, doomed if you don't." He did
have a point.

No matter what choice I made, I would not be happy. If
I chose to go home, I would feel like a complete failure and
would never be able to look my mother in the eye again. If I
chose to continue with the assignment, I would probably lose
my life and never see my mother again, leaving her without
any family and breaking her heart.

"Maybe you should start taking matters into your
own hands. Demand what you want. Demand that you be
allowed to go home and not labeled as a traitor or coward,"
he continued. "You have a right to be happy."

I couldn't help but start to agree with him more and
more as he spoke. "You know, maybe I should. I do have the
right to be happy and do what I want. Hey, what's your name
anyway?"

"I go by many names." He smiled slyly but did not
answer me. He stopped walking. "It's time for me to leave
you know. I think you'll be safe now. Remember to demand
what you want. You are entitled to that. Until we meet again
. . ." With that he was gone. Vanished in a puff of smoke. I
wondered if I had even really seen him there at all.

The fog began to clear, just enough that the road finally stopped moving beneath my feet. My head was pounding. I couldn't think straight. I needed to lie down. I looked around for a place to rest and saw that I hadn't left the fountain. Had I made up the encounter?

I managed to stagger back up to the palace and went in through the servant's door. I wasn't in the mood to run into anyone. Sneaking through the passageways I made my way to my chambers without incident.

By the time I laid down on my bed, I couldn't bear the pain in my head. I tried to sleep, but it alluded me. When I realized the throbbing was not easing at all, I decided to go find the physician. Maybe he would be able to give me something to ease the pain, or at least help me sleep through it.

It took me much longer than normal to reach the physician's door. I had been there several times to have minor injuries treated from training and knew the way well, but this time I had to stop every few feet to let the pain clear enough for me to see straight. From inside the doctor's room I could hear muffled protest in response to my pounding. I could hear his talons scraping across the floor, and it seemed to take forever for him to answer. When the door finally opened, Regi seemed as if he were about to let me have it, but after he looked at me, his reptilian eyes grew large and he quickly pulled me in and asked me what on Mythica was wrong.

I was about to tell him, then hesitated. I wasn't sure if what happened was real or if I had imagined it all. For all I knew, I could have fallen and hit my head, and that could have been the reason I hallucinated. Instead, I just told him the symptoms.

He went to a table that had all sorts of plants on it. His tail curling around him allowed him to move more easily. He pulled off leaves from several of them and began putting them in a bowl of boiling water. It wasn't long before he came over with the bowl and told me to drink. I was in so much pain I didn't even question what he had given me; instead, I gulped the entire contents of the bowl down. The water burned my throat. It tasted like something Shilla had charred from the depths of the sea, but the potion worked quickly, and for that I was grateful.

Drowsiness began to take over, and the last thing I remembered before falling asleep was Regi's human-like face peering over mine, its scale-covered surface scrunched in concern.

CHAPTER SIX

The Team

"WELL, IT'S ABOUT TIME YOU WOKE UP." I could still feel the weight of unconscious around me. My eyes were heavy to lift.

I couldn't remember much of what happened before I passed out. I had gone out to the city to clear my head, and I was looking into the pond. After that, everything was blank.

Looking around I realized I was in the medical ward. I hadn't been in this room yet. The soldiers brought here often came straight from the battlefields.

Regi was standing across the room wrapping gauze around another soldier. A few others were lying in beds, their conditions ranging from minor cuts to lost limbs. I tried not to think about what had caused such injuries.

I attempted to sit up but was forced back down by a splitting pain in my head. It felt as if someone had taken a hammer and swung it at my head with all the force of a Mountain Ogre. Upon hearing my groan Regi quickly made his way to my bed, his tongue slithering with displeasure.

"You need to stay lying down for a bit. Do you remember anything of what happened last night?" He frowned when I shook my head. "I was afraid of that. You were injected with a pretty strong poison. I had hoped you would be able to tell me how you came into contact with it. In the meantime, you need to stay as still as possible. I have managed to get what I could of the poison out of your system. Now we just need to let the antidote take effect."

He held up a glass of water to my lips and forced me to take a few sips. Without saying another word, he scurried back over to the patient he had been attending.

What in Mythica happened to me last night? It concerned me that I couldn't remember how I got back to the palace. Who had tried to poison me? And why? The pounding in my head began to get stronger again, and I closed my eyes to try and fight it off.

"Be careful, Zalan." It was Elyon again. After years of wanting Him to answer me, I was beginning to ever regret doing so. I tried ignoring Him, but He continued. *"There are many dark forces on Mythica, and they want to turn you from the truth I have set before you. They will do anything in their power to keep you from becoming who you are meant to be."*

Truth? Who I'm meant to be? Why must you always talk in riddles? He completely ignored my questions. *"Going against these dark creatures will not be like any other battle. You will need to rely on more than just your own physical strength to get you through."*

Fight something without using physical strength. You mean with cunning and smarts instead?

"No, my son, you will need much more than that."

I am not *Your son, and I would prefer You not to call me that.* That sparked something in my mind. Someone else had been calling be something I wasn't. Brother? Son? Friend?

I didn't have time to ponder it further. Regi was back, telling me I should be able to sit up now. He claimed the poison was gone, but my mind still felt foggy. Regi was speaking, but his voice sounded muffled, almost as if he were underwater. He was pushing a bowl into my hands. He didn't seem concerned that I wasn't fully alert, or maybe he just didn't notice.

The contents of the bowl reminded me of home. It was

the one meal Mother made Helia every day when she was sick: potato soup. The warm broth felt so good going down my throat. The comfort of the food was lulling me back to sleep. I had just managed to drink the last little bit before the tendrils of dreams overtook me once more.

It was the same dream I had been having every night at the palace, although things were slightly different this time. The beast in the shadow had taken on a more definite shape. It resembled a lion, but there was something else still obscured by the shadows. The name of the beast came to my mind. Belial. Without a doubt I knew it to be true. This was the sworn enemy of Elyon Himself. Why was he terrifying me in my dreams?

Talia was no longer trying to get me to run. Instead, when I looked over my shoulder to see her, the intense look I had seen in her eyes in the study was there. She seemed to want to face Belial head-on. It was a futile fight. She would lose before it even began.

She was saying something, but I couldn't quite make it out. I was finally able to hear her after her mouth stopped moving. The sound seemed to be traveling through a thick substance in the air, slowing it down.

"Zalan, do not run away in fear. Elyon has given us what we need to fight. All you need to do is look for it within yourself." What did that mean? I turned to look back at the shadow lion. The grin he wore was terrifying.

"Yes, Zalan. Stand and fight. See how long you can survive against me. I would love to devour you whole. Cowards are my favorite." His voice dripped with honey despite the venom his words held. He was right. The only chance of surviving I had was to run. I couldn't face him. To try would be certain death.

The shadow began to creep closer. It followed the movements of the lion, not giving us the chance to see what the lion hid. Belial's claws scraped against the ground, the sound so piercing I wondered if my ears would bleed. Just like all the other times before, I ran.

When I didn't hear the screams that always came, I looked back to see Talia fighting the shadow instead of being overtaken by it. But she wasn't strong enough. She wasn't going to win. I had to make the decision to go back and help her or to continue to run like the coward I seemed to be.

I didn't have the chance to make that decision. I woke up to someone shaking my shoulders. The deep furrow in Paladin's brow made me wonder if I had been asleep for much longer than it had felt like I had. He must have guessed at my thoughts, for he assured me only an hour had passed since I was last awake. But he did say I had been screaming in my sleep.

"Is everything all right? You had us really worried. Regi sent word of your condition as quickly as he could. He says you have been in contact with a very poisonous substance. Can you remember anything that happened?" His brows furrowed even deeper, and there was a hint of anger I had never seen there before. Paladin never seemed to get angry.

When I shook my head, he walked across the room and stood by the window, staring out with a pained look. I wished I had the ability to guess what he was thinking and feeling. "Lord Paladin, what is it that troubles you so?"

He took in a deep breath and held it for far longer than I expected was comfortable before exhaling just as strongly. "I am afraid you have been bitten by a snake whose poison is unique. If my fears are realized, then we are more in need of the Armor than first thought." He sighed once more. "Belial and I used to play together when we lived in Highland. We shared many laughs. However, his lust for the same power as Elyon began to grow. It was consuming him, changing him. I had no other choice than to inform my father of this, although Elyon already knew. He called Belial to him and cursed him, then banished him from ever entering Highland again. Belial has never forgiven us."

His eyes began to fill with tears, just for a moment, before hardening once more. "Belial had been my friend once, but friend he is no longer. He has tried to hurt my people and take control over their life. He has been slowly succeeding. The seeds he planted in others have grown like weeds among the people. They are no longer heeding my words. I am losing the faith of the people, and Belial thinks he is winning. I believe he poisoned you as well." He turned to look at me. "You truly have no recollection of encountering anyone last night?"

"I'm sorry, Lord Paladin, I can't remember anything after sitting down by the fountain."

"If you recall anything, please send word to me immediately. If Belial has grown so brave as to infiltrate my city . . ." His fists balled up at his sides before releasing them again.

I had never seen Paladin this upset.

"Zalan, I pray to Elyon that you heal quickly. You will need all the strength you have, and more, to survive the coming days." He turned back to the window. "There will come a day when the people of Mythica will no longer welcome me. Their eyes will be covered from the truth and they will throw me out. That day is not far away."

He turned to me, and the sadness I saw caused tears to come to my own eyes. He genuinely thought the people he cared so much about would turn on him. Despite my dislike of his father, I had grown to trust and honor Paladin. To think of the people turning on him was, well, it was unthinkable.

He closed his eyes, and when he opened them again, the sadness was replaced with a determination. "Zalan, you are needed on the field. Regi believes all the poison has left and you are ready to resume your training. If Belial is getting bold enough to enter the city, we will need the Armor as quickly as possible. I am sorry to rush you. You and your team do not have much time to prepare."

His determination was so strong I could feel it seeping into my own feelings. Without another word I stood from the bed and bowed. The fog and pain had completely disappeared. All thoughts of the nightmare were gone. With that, I ran to the training field.

The other four had already paired off and were fighting in hand-to-hand combat. No one had noticed my arrival so I decided to sit back and watch for a moment.

These soldiers had been trained well. They all moved with such fluid movements that, not for the first time, I wondered why I had been assigned to this mission. My skills may have improved greatly, but compared to what I was witnessing, they were still rudimentary at best.

To my dismay it appeared that Sir Gael had been placed as leader of our mission. He spotted me watching the others and called out, "You finally make it to practice and all you are doing is standing there. Afraid you are going to get hurt?"

Everyone stopped what they were doing and turned toward me. My cheeks burned, but I held his gaze and stood taller. I would not let this high and mighty Elven get the better of me.

"I was merely observing my comrades' techniques to better master them, sir." I tried not to spit out the words, but by the way his eyes narrowed I wasn't sure I had succeeded.

"Then let us see how well you have observed." His tone was even. "Julio, grab your sword. You and Zalan will battle, and do not go easy."

I pulled my sword from my scabbard and walked to the center of the field. This was not the first time I had been underestimated. I would show Sir Gael, just like I showed Commander Briggen, what I was capable of. I needed to prove myself, to show that I could be a valuable member of the team, not only to Sir Gael, but to myself as well.

Julio came and stood across from me. I knew instantly why Sir Gael had picked him. He was the largest of the team, towering a foot higher than me and twice as wide. I had watched enough of his fighting to know he was good, really good. I would be lying if I said I wasn't intimidated. That very truth made me all the more determined. I had a small chance of beating him, but I would not go down without a fight.

I was waiting for Sir Gael to tell us to begin, but he didn't, and I was down on the ground before I could figure out what had happened. It was just like the first day when I was fighting Jeg. Sir Gael laughed, then shouted something about always being ready. In a real battle there was not someone telling you when to begin.

I could feel my anger rise. I quickly got to my feet before Julio could charge again. I watched him for a moment, trying to get a read on him. His eyes were filled with confidence. He knew he would win. That gave me a little bit of hope. Since he thought the match was already his, he wouldn't give his all, despite Sir Gael telling him not to go easy. I would use that to my advantage.

The next time he charged I swept to the side in the last moment and sliced his front leg. It was a good thing we were still using dull blades that would leave nothing but a bruise.

Julio turned quickly toward me, surprise written all over his face. I had gained the upper hand. In a real fight that move would have cost him his leg, causing him to have to fight with just three. That should have meant the fight was over, but Sir Gael didn't say anything. He just watched us with a smile curled on his lips. He would have us fight until one of us was down on the ground. I ground my teeth and squared my shoulders. So be it.

I had lost the advantage, and despite getting in a couple more hits, Julio bested me. I was on the ground face-first, the taste of dirt in my mouth. I could feel one of his hooves on my back while another pinned my hand down, keeping me from using my sword.

"Enough. Well done, Julio." Sir Gael didn't say anything to me, he just wore a smug smile. It didn't escape my notice that his eyes seemed to dance with intrigue as he looked back to me. Something I had done had caught his attention. If only I knew what.

Looking around at the faces of Julio, Talia, Kitsune, and Sage, I knew I had gained some respect among them. They must have seen my puzzled expression, for Kitsune answered my unasked question.

"You might not have won, but you fought well. Not very many people can last that long against Julio, not even Sir Gael, although you will never hear him admit it."

Sir Gael huffed, then barked orders to pair up and spar.

Julio turned to me. "I see you and Sir Gael have a bit of history. We have been under his command for not more than a day, and it appears he already has it out for you." His deep, dry voice had a hint of laughter in it, causing me to relax slightly

"He and I have an understanding of each other." A coy smile slipped its way to my lips. Julio hmphed, then laughed, the wrinkles on his dry skin deepening.

"Julio did not hurt you too badly, I hope." Talia's voice held the silver sound of bells. My breath caught as it brought the image of her fighting the shadow. "Is your mouth so full of dirt that you cannot speak?" Her smile was a surprise. At the meeting with Paladin she seemed so intense and focused. I didn't expect her to be one for lightheartedness.

"He must have knocked me down harder than I thought. I saw you guys fighting earlier. Did you learn all that just while in palace training?" I was trying for small talk, but her reaction was not what I had expected. Her smile vanished and turned into a tight line, while her eyes glimmered with what? Anger? Sadness? I couldn't tell what had caused a shadow to pass over them. I was about to apologize for whatever I had said when Julio's hand came up on my shoulder, stopping me. Talia turned and stalked away toward Kitsune, who promptly began to spar with her.

"Talia has trained with some of the greatest fighters known to Mythica, and anyone else who will take the time to work with her." Julio's voice held a deep sadness. "Her family was overtaken by Belial's forces and his shadow has overtaken her entire land, causing everyone to freeze as statues, their souls no longer inside them. Talia was one of the only few to escape that fate, and she has vowed to do everything in her power to destroy Belial and free her people."

"I didn't know." How could someone who has lost so much still follow Elyon? I had lost just two people in my life and held so much resentment toward Him. To lose everyone I loved? That was something I knew I could not bear.

"Do not take it personally. The next time you two interact she will pretend as if nothing happened. I advise you to do the same." I looked up at Julio to see him watching her. Such sadness filled his eyes.

"How do you know so much about her? Especially since she doesn't seem to like to talk about it."

"Talia and I met shortly after she lost her family. We trained under the same master for a while. We quickly became friends, and I agreed to travel with her."

The same shadow that passed Talia's eyes now passed his. I could tell there was more to it than that. I wondered if the same thing that happened to Talia's people also happened to his.

Sir Gael came up to us and asked if we planned on standing around gossiping all day. I wanted nothing more than to tell him I loved to stand around and gossip just to spite him, but I held my tongue.

Sir Gael knew how to train a team. By days end I had managed to learn how each of the members preferred to fight, even if I wasn't able to defeat any of them. I spent all that night thinking about their moves, and by the next day I was able to deflect their attacks more frequently.

Kitsune, just like the Three-Tailed Foxes that lived in our village, held true to her people and, despite her cute appearance, was very cunning. She knew just how to keep you focused on one thing long enough that you didn't see the real attack coming. She was the hardest one for me to fight against.

Julio's strength outmatched all the others, and he knew it, but his cockiness always allowed me to get in a few blows.

Talia's fighting styles varied the most. There was no denying she had been trained by many different skilled fighters. I had yet to make a successful attack against her.

Sage was a much easier opponent, which made my victory against her less rewarding, but I had a feeling she used her weakness as a shield, hiding behind it until it was time to strike. A fire in her eyes told me there was more to her than she was letting on.

And then there was Sir Gael. Because there was an odd number of us, we each had our turn fighting him. He was stronger and quicker than one would think for his age. His Elven limbs gave him a longer reach with his swords. He was the only one in the group who fought with two. None of us had yet to best him.

We all went to the dining hall together, but when we arrived, I made my way over to Jeg instead of eating with the others. I needed to tell him all that had occurred.

"Salutation, Zalan."

"Hey, Jeg. Sorry I haven't been around lately."

"No storms, although I was configuring why you poofed."

I would sure miss his use of words. I sat down at the table next to him and told him all that happened, at least all I could remember. I watched as concern and sadness crept into his expression. His eyes misted over, and his wooden features bunched together. My own throat closed with emotion. I realized then that I would miss Jeg. He had become a true friend to me while at the palace. I expressed as much to him, and he returned the sentiment. It felt like leaving Shilla behind all over again.

***

When the day to depart arrived we all met in Paladin's study. He wanted to give us one last farewell and to make sure we were equipped with everything we needed.

"Our scouts say Belial's shadows have been spotted in the heart of Pixie Forest."

Talia made a grunting noise, and when I glanced over, she looked as if she had swallowed something sour.

"We believe that is where he has hidden one of the pieces of the Armor and placed it under guard. That is where you will begin." He stopped and looked at each one of us, peering into our faces. "Remember, Elyon is with you and will guide you. Open your hearts and let Him in. He will do amazing things if only you give Him the chance."

The way he said it made me feel like I was not the only one who doubted Elyon's goodness. I couldn't help but wonder who else might be harboring hatred toward Him. Talia was the most likely, but I had seen her pray to Elyon several times in the few days we had been together.

"Elyon be with you all as you go on the path He has set before you."

When everyone else began to leave the room, Paladin pulled me aside, which earned me some curious glances from the others.

"Zalan, I know you still do not see your role in this mission, but in the coming days it will be shown to you. The strength you will need is more than you have, and the burden will be greater than you can carry."

"Paladin, if I won't have the strength I need, then why are you putting me in this situation? Why would Elyon set me up to fail?"

"My dear Zalan, Elyon is not setting you up to fail. He is setting you up for greatness. Now, you must get going. The others are waiting. Be careful whom you trust."

That was it? I would be given no further explanation? I was certain I was being sent out to die, and there wasn't anything I could do to stop it, except fight. I would show Elyon that I wouldn't live by His will. I would show Him I really did have the strength to handle whatever He decided to throw at me, all on my own.

I jumped in shock when I saw Kitsune on the other side of the door. I figured she had gone with the others already. Apparently she wanted to overhear my conversation with Paladin instead.

"What did Paladin tell you?" Her eyes felt like drills. Something flashed in them that made me pause before answering. *Be careful whom you trust.* Was someone in our group a spy? Surely Paladin would have known this and not placed them on this mission. Still, I didn't tell her the truth, just to be cautious.

"He just wanted to wish me luck on the mission is all." I forced a laugh. "I guess he thinks I need more of it than you guys."

Her eyes narrowed just for a moment before she smiled

and walked away.

CHAPTER SEVEN

Encounter

AFTER THE MEETING WITH PALADIN I walked back to my chambers to gather my things. I once more pulled the picture from beneath my pillow. I thought back on the day I left to come to the palace. Those emotions of hate, anger, and fear all came rushing back. I could feel the tendrils of darkness start to creep around the edges of my mind.

I squeezed my eyes shut, trying to push back the darkness. I refused to be overcome. The last thing I wanted was for one of my new team to find me blacked out. I pushed against the dark force and slowly the shadows began to recede. I let out a huge sigh and slumped onto the bed.

I sat there for a few moments waiting for my breathing to go back to normal. It took a lot out of me to fight back.

Once my nerves were steady once more, I went over to the desk and began to write home, not knowing when I would again get the chance.

Dear Shilla,

I only have time for one letter, so please pass along this news to Mother.

I can't wait until the day we are all together again. I wish I knew when that day will be.

Paladin has given me a special assignment. That's right. Yours truly is going on what you could call a quest.

Apparently there is some magical armor that's supposed to save all of Mythica, and my team is being sent to find it. I am excited to go explore the rest of Mythica, I never thought I would get to do that, although (and don't tell Mother of this) I'm afraid more than ever that I won't return home. Paladin says this mission is extremely dangerous. His eyes held a glint of sadness that made me wonder if he is knowingly sending us to our death.

I wish I could write and tell more, but time is running short. We are leaving today. Know that I may not be able to send word for quite some time, but I promise I will the moment I am able.

Love your dearest friend,

Zalan

No sooner had I finished sealing the letter than a knock came at my door.

"I'll be right out."

I quickly picked up my picture from where it had fallen against the bed. Placing it in my bag, I looked to see what I was missing. My gaze landed on my copy of the Text. I had placed it on my bedside table and hadn't touched it once since arriving. I thought for a moment about leaving it behind. I even started to walk out the door without it, but something caused me to turn back and quickly pack it away.

I opened the door, not sure if I would ever return to this room again.

"It is about time. Everyone is waiting at the palace steps." Maggi was zipping back and forth, eager to be on her way.

"Let the others know I'll be right dow—" Before I could finish my sentence she was gone. I followed behind her, but at a much more reluctant pace. I wasn't ready to face whatever was before me.

***

The suns were already halfway across their path when we approached the grove of trees where we would spend the night. Everyone had remained silent up until then, only speaking when they needed to. The reality of our situation had finally caught up with us. We might not find the Armor. We might not make it back home. The only sound that could be heard for quite some time was the sound of our horses and Julio's hooves hitting the ground.

As we neared the trees the others began speaking more easily. The conversations were less forced. The only one who remained silent was Talia. I watched as her shoulders seemed to tighten with every step. She appeared to be more agitated than the rest.

I brought my horse up to her own. "Are you not excited to stop for the night and rest?"

"What do you mean?" She tried to smile, but it came out more like a grimace.

"You look pretty tense, as if you are not happy we are stopping."

She sighed heavily, her shoulders lowering as she did. "It is not that I don't want to rest. It's just that I would much rather get through Pixie Forest and be done with it."

"What do you have against the forest?"

"It is not the forest I have an issue with, it is the Pixies. Fairies do not get along very well with them. Pixies are known for being cruel and setting traps just for pleasure. They like pranking, not caring how much they hurt someone. They give Fairies a bad name. People always assume Fairies and Pixies are the same because we are cousins, but we are nothing like them. Never would we bring ourselves that low." The anger behind her words told me there was more to her personal hatred toward them.

"I know as a follower of Paladin I should not feel that way toward any creature. It's just that Pixies make it so hard not to despise them. They really do not care what people think of them and do such horrible things."

We both fell into silence. I looked up to see how much farther we still needed to go. Kitsune quickly turned back around. She had been watching us. The air around me seemed to get a little colder. For some reason Kitsune had gotten into a habit of listening in on my conversations. I would need to watch her a little more carefully.

We were just on the outskirts of the trees, the moons casting long shadows across the ground, when Sir Gael finally pulled his horse to a stop. "We rest here."

There was a collective sigh of relief from everyone.

Sir Gael's lip turned up slightly. "The last thing I need is for all of you to get killed because you are exhausted." He dismounted and immediately started barking orders.

Kitsune and I were sent to get firewood. Hopefully it would be the perfect time to get some answers from her.

She came leaping over to me and looked me up and down before trotting off just within the tree line. I had to run to catch up with her.

"Kitsune, why were you watching Talia and me earlier?"

"It is no secret there is something between you two. I saw it the first day we met in Paladin's study. You were shocked to see her, as if you knew her. Yet you act as if the two of you have never met. She does the same." I hadn't realized it was that obvious, nor did I know Talia had been acting the same way. Then I remembered her eyes watching me that first day. Did she have dreams about *me*? Or was it something else entirely?

"You two have a bond of some kind and I am just trying to figure out why."

She looked over at me. I knew she wanted me to tell her

why I seemed to know Talia, but I couldn't. I didn't know if it was safe. Besides, I still didn't know what it all meant, and I wasn't sure I wanted to tell anyone before I had it figured out.

When I didn't answer her right away, she turned and started picking up twigs with her mouth. Her pointed nose lifted the heavier ones before she grabbed them within her teeth. I wanted to ask her why she had been outside Paladin's study, but I didn't want her to know I suspected anything. I watched her carefully out of the corner of my eye. If she were to tighten her jaw, those sticks would snap with ease. I really hoped she could be trusted. If she were on the enemy's side, we would all be in serious trouble, and possibly lose some limbs.

I was just bending down to grab a few small sticks when I heard a sound. Somewhere off in the distance something had moved. Kitsune's hearing was far more acute than my own, but she didn't appear to have heard anything. She cocked her head at me when I motioned for her to remain quiet. A twig snapped. This time the sound came from the opposite direction.

"There you are, Zalan. I've been looking all over for you." A shadow stepped from behind a tree.

"Who are you?"

"You do not remember me? I am hurt. You are my friend, after all." I wondered if Kitsune could see him too, or if once more my mind was playing tricks on me.

Friend. Images of this man walking with me in the city. Calling me his friend. It all came back to me now in a rush. He was the same one in the shadow of my dreams. This man in front of me was Belial himself. My head was pounding from the realization.

"Ah, I see you remember who I am now. It is so good to see you again."

"What do you want from me?" I snapped.

"So harsh." He made a show of grabbing at his heart. "And here I was just trying to give you some good news." His lips curled in a smile, those sharp teeth once more showing themselves.

I looked to see if Kitsune was just as uneasy as I was, but she wasn't there. Where did she go?

"Do you not want to know what news I have to share?"

I still didn't respond. My tongue was like sandpaper in my mouth.

"Oh well, I will tell you anyway. I found someone who has long been absent from your life."

My mouth grew even dryer. Who could he possibly be talking about?

"Your father."

All the blood drained from my body. It couldn't be true. It was impossible.

"My father has been dead for years." My voice was barely a whisper.

"Has he? He looked pretty alive to me. Are you sure he was really dead? I mean, did they ever find his body?"

A seed of doubt and hope began to sprout inside of me. When I didn't answer Belial smiled again. Victory shown in his eyes. He knew he had me.

"Your father is safe at my palace. He is very eager to see you again."

"Why didn't he come and find me himself?"

"He wanted to, but he was quite injured from his trials. He sent me to bring you to him instead."

"How do I know I can trust you? You poisoned me, remember, Belial?" I spat his name.

"I see you've figured out my name. Good for you." A hissing sound came from somewhere behind him. His face tensed for just a moment before he continued. "That poison didn't come from me. I would never harm you. Not like the others you have blindly put your trust in."

"What are you talking about?"

"How well do you know Paladin? How can you be sure he was not the one who poisoned you, then turned around and placed the blame on me to cover up his tracks. He knew your father was alive all this time, and he chose to keep it from you. How can you trust a man like that?"

He knew? Why didn't he say anything to me?

"If you do not believe me, you can come to the palace and see for yourself that your father is alive. He will tell you the truth. Paladin is not to be trusted."

I wasn't sure if I could trust Belial no matter what he told me, but I knew one thing for sure: I had to find out if my father really was alive.

"How do I know you won't attack me or keep me prisoner?"

"If I wanted to harm you, I would have all ready."

He had a point. Belial had plenty of opportunities to capture me or harm me, but he hadn't.

"Then let's go."

"Unfortunately I cannot take you to him right away. I have some unfinished business to attend to. But not to worry, stay with your little group of misfits and you will soon find your way to my palace. There is someone among you whom I trust. When the time is right, they will show you the way. Farewell, Zalan. Until we meet again."

He was gone as quickly as he came.

"Zalan!."

I blinked in surprise. Kitsune was back, her jaw poised to strike.

"What are you doing?" I quickly moved out of her reach. "Where did you run off to?"

She tilted her head in puzzlement. "I did not go anywhere. You are the one who is acting strangely. It was as if you had totally spaced out. I was about to bite you to snap you out of it. What happened to you?"

She really didn't know? How could she not have seen Belial standing right there? For all I knew she was putting on an act and was really working with Belial. Or maybe she was working with Paladin and was making sure I didn't find out the truth about my father.

"It must be the remnants of that poison I came into contact with. I'm okay now. I promise. Let's get back to camp. I'm sure they're wondering what happened to us by now."

She had a doubtful look in her eyes but didn't question me further. Neither of us spoke the rest of the way back to the camp, but I could feel Kitsune glancing at me every few steps.

How long was I supposed to wait for "the right time"? Belial was no better than Paladin in causing more questions than answers. I wasn't sure how much longer I could take it. And who was the one Belial trusted?

CHAPTER EIGHT

Belial, Again

ZALAN IS PROVING TO BE AN EASIER PREY than I imagined. I was able to pull the strings of doubt like an expert puppeteer. It is all too easy.

He will soon find his way to my palace in search of his father. By then I will know the truth. After all these years of waiting and searching, I have found him, and I will destroy him.

"My lord, what if we usssed him to help usss inssstead?"

"Yes, my lord, that sounds like such a marvelous idea. He could be persuaded to fight *for* us."

"Hmmm." These fools might be good for something after all. "That does indeed sound like a good plan. In the meantime, we have business to tend to in Grand Thial. It's high time you two were uncovered for a little bit."

Lord Paladin would regret ever getting me kicked out from Highland.

CHAPTER NINE

The First Battle

SIR GAEL HAD US UP AND MOVING before daylight had broken. I could tell by the looks on my comrades' faces that none of us had slept very well. The ground had been a rude awakening to the comfort we had been enjoying back at the palace. It didn't help that I kept thinking about Belial and whether I could really trust him. He could have been lying about my father, but I couldn't come up with a reason why. I had no choice but to go to his palace and find out the truth.

Kitsune had informed the others of what happened to me in the forest. I wasn't too pleased with her announcing to the world that I had spaced out. Thankfully they all believed it was the effects of the poison, but I couldn't help but notice how they all began to look at me with sympathy or worry. I didn't want them to think I was weak and some kind of burden to them, but I couldn't tell them the truth of what happened either. Sir Gael was the only one who didn't look at me oddly or treat me differently. He was still barking orders at me and giving me the toughest jobs.

By the time the second sun was fully above the horizon, we reached Pixie Forest. Everyone seemed to be holding their breath in anticipation of what we would find. I looked over to Talia to see her knuckles were white, gripping the reigns of her horse.

"All right, team. Stay close and keep your eyes open. A piece of the Armor is supposed to be in this forest somewhere.

We must find it at all costs."

We dismounted our horses and followed Sir Gael into the trees. After just a few feet in, the light became just a dim haze. The only light flickered through the leaves, causing the shadows to dance along the ground.

The weight of so many secrets and distrust was beginning to settle on my shoulders. The pressure felt familiar. It was the same burden I had carried ever since the day my father left. I hadn't noticed its absence until it was back, but I recognized the feeling. It was the weight of being alone and unwanted, of loss and regrets, only it was even heavier.

I was so lost in thought I didn't notice Sage had come up next to me. "Hey, is everything okay? You seem pretty distracted today."

Up to that point Sage had been distant toward me. She seemed to prefer the company of Kitsune, but other than that she kept pretty much to herself. I couldn't help but wonder why she would take notice of me now. The seed of suspicion grew larger inside me.

"I'm fine. I guess I was thinking about all Paladin had said about the Armor and what it's capable of." I hated that I was lying more and more, but I didn't see another choice.

"It is pretty amazing how Elyon would create something so powerful to help us. He could have let us fight on our own, but instead He has taken an interest in our lives and helps us, if we let Him. Like Paladin said, we need to open our hearts and let Elyon work within us."

I didn't say anything. Sage seemed to want to continue the conversation, but the last thing I wanted to talk about was Elyon. I had let Him in once, and He betrayed me. I wouldn't make the same mistake again.

"Zalan, have you learned to let Elyon in, truly in?"

When I didn't respond she just made a hmmming sound before taking her place next to Kitsune once more. I watched as they whispered to one another, occasionally looking back at me. Once again, the feeling of distrust grew, and so did the weight on my shoulders. I didn't like it when people talked about me, especially when it had to do with my choice not to follow Elyon. My anger was brewing up inside me. I hadn't felt it this strong in quite some time. I took a deep breath and was about to let all my frustration out on Sage and Kitsune, but before I could, something snapped underneath my foot.

I didn't have time to register the fact it wasn't a simple twig before I was flung into the air. Blood rushed to my head as I swung upside down from a rope firmly wrapped around my ankles. The twirling motion was causing my stomach to sour.

A few surprised gasps came from those I traveled with, followed by some chuckles. Those sounds were replaced with metal scraping. The others had drawn their swords. The twirling was beginning to slow down, but I was still going around too fast to see why they had taken up arms.

When I was finally able to focus, I still couldn't see what they were fighting against. It looked as if they were swinging their swords at thin air. Then I glimpsed one of the attackers. Just the tiniest reflection from the sun. It was the Pixies. They were moving so fast it was as if they weren't even there.

The look of hatred on Talia's face confirmed what I was seeing. Her thin jaw was tight with rage. The others were holding off the Pixies, but just barely. I needed to find a way out of the trap, and quickly.

Using all the strength I had, I curled my top half up to my feet. Grabbing hold of the rope with one hand, I was able to keep myself folded in half while reaching for the dagger I had hidden in my boot with the other hand, since my sword had fallen from my waist when I was turned upside down. I sawed at the rope until it finally gave away. By how long I fell and how hard the impact was, I determined I must have been much higher up than I'd thought.

My vision blurred for just a moment and I was pretty sure I heard something crack, but I didn't have time to figure out what.

"He's loose! Watch him!" a Pixie yelled.

It sounded like they were right next to me, but when I turned, no one was there. I couldn't see them attacking, but I could feel their weapons hitting me. I began swinging rapidly, hoping to catch one of them by sheer luck.

"Zalan! Behind you."

Talia's warning came just in time. I spun out of the way as her dagger flew past where my head would have been and hit its mark. I heard a loud thud and looked to see the fallen Pixie. A large red splotch was growing wider with each passing second. He was already gone. I didn't know how Talia had been able to see him, but I was thankful she had. The sword he was carrying was so large I would have been killed with one blow.

"Thank me later." Talia spun back around to fight another enemy I couldn't see.

How was I supposed to fight something nearly invisible? They were even faster than Maggi. I couldn't wait for the sun to reflect in just the right position to reveal them again. I had to start swinging, hoping I would catch one. I was quickly realizing the training I'd received at the palace was just the basics. I still had a great deal yet to learn. I only hopped I would survive long enough to get the chance.

Talia must have noticed my struggle. She called over her shoulder while still maintaining her strikes against her opponent. "Listen for the sound of their wings. You can hear them flapping. This battle is one of the ears, not the eyes."

I closed my eyes to listen. She was right. It was faint, but there. Moving by sheer muscle memory, I began attacking. I could feel it when my dagger struck and heard the screams of pain I inflicted.

When I couldn't hear the sound of their wings anymore, I opened my eyes. To my surprise there must have been twenty Pixies scattered on the ground, several of them dead. I turned to look at the team and found them all staring at me.

Shock, surprise, and awe were on their faces. "Why are you all looking at me like that?" I asked.

"Do you not realize what you just did?" Even Sir Gael looked at me with amazement, and a hint of pride.

"Zalan, when I said to listen to their wings, I did not mean for you to close your eyes while you were fighting." Talia's voice had a slight edge, her eyes narrowing ever so slightly. What could I have done to make her upset with me?

"You still do not realize what happened, do you?" Kitsune's eyes were wide in shock. "You took out half of the Pixies in a matter of minutes."

Surely she was exaggerating. I couldn't have possibly been responsible for stopping that many. Could I? "That's impossible. I'm not that skilled. You all have far more experience than I do. Surely you guys attacked more of them than you thought."

"No, Zalan. You fought amazingly well. I didn't know you could fight like that." Sage was shaking her head in disbelief. I was sure if she kept up, it would eventually snap off.

"Well, there is no point in standing around gawking. Paladin knew he was placing people with all sorts of different skills together. Now we know Zalan's skill is fighting with his eyes closed." Julio's voice was calm, but there was a calculating look in his eyes. He kept glancing between Talia and me, as if he was trying to decide something. "We still have the piece of Armor to find, and seeing as we were attacked by the Pixies with no obvious cause, we must be getting close. Would you not agree, Sir Gael?"

Sir Gael agreed with Julio and ordered us to interrogate

any Pixie still alive and demand they tell us why they had engaged in a full-blown fight without any provocation and reveal anything they knew of the Armor.

Everyone followed his command, and I was relieved their eyes no longer bore into me. I couldn't believe I had caused so much of this devastation. The others had obviously been impressed, yet I didn't feel the infliction of death and injury was something to be congratulated for. Knowing I had taken the life of so many made me sick to my stomach. I knew the pain that death left behind. Even if the Pixies had initiated the fight, I couldn't help but think of the families left to deal with the loss of the lives I took.

Taking a few paces away I hid behind a tree and dispelled everything I had in my stomach. Suddenly laughter came from deep within the trees. I snapped my head and looked around to see who had made the sound. No one else seemed to have heard it.

I heard the laughter again, and this time felt the urge to follow it. My feet began to move forward before I could command them to. The source of the laughter remained just out of sight, only occurring again when I began to wonder if I'd heard it at all. It was leading me deep into the forest. When I turned to see how far I had gone, I was shocked I could see the others, as if I was still right behind the tree, yet when I looked ahead I was now standing at the edge of a meadow.

The field was covered in wildflowers so tall they reached my waist. Something was odd about them. They all faced the center of the meadow, toward a giant tree bigger than any other in the forest. The roots were larger than the thickness of my body, maybe even Commander Briggen's.

The laughter came again. It was coming from the tree. I knew I should return to the others, but when I went to turn around, I couldn't. My body wouldn't listen to my commands. Instead, it began walking to the tree.

The air changed the moment I stepped into the outcropping. It was thicker, warmer, strange. I could see a breeze pushing the leaves of the tree and the flowers around me, but I couldn't feel it.

I looked down to see that my feet hadn't left the ground trampled. It was as if I wasn't walking on it at all. If something were to happen to me, no one would be able to tell where I had gone. Despite the warmth of the air, a shiver ran down my spine and the hair on my arms stood on end. I knew I shouldn't be there, yet I felt a strange desire to stay.

When I walked underneath the leaves of the tree, the laughter suddenly stopped. I sensed someone or something watching me. I looked around but didn't see anything. The tree appeared to almost shimmer. Taking a step closer I saw it was moving, growing so quickly I could see the bark stretching. My hand was about to reach out for it when a voice startled me.

"Be careful. This place does not feel natural." I must have jumped because a chuckle escape Talia's lips.

"Did you follow me here?" I tried to hide my irritation at her laughter.

"I saw you walking away from the rest of the group. You had a strange look on your face, and after your reaction to the fight, I wanted to make sure you were okay." Her eye twitched slightly.

Was she lying? I didn't remember seeing her behind me when I looked back, but if her intent was not to be seen, then she would have succeeded. But why would she need to hide if she was merely checking on me? Maybe she held the same suspicions of our group as I did, or maybe she was the one who couldn't be trusted. I felt trapped in the box of distrust. It was shrinking more and more, beginning to suffocate me. Maybe the reason Talia had not been overtaken from the shadow was because she was now working with it.

"Why did you come out here?"

Talia's question pulled me from my thoughts. Seeing that same look of sympathy on her face from earlier was a blow to the gut.

"I heard something and thought I would come check it out. Then I saw this tree and couldn't believe how big it was. Guess I wanted to get a closer look." I couldn't help but give half-truths. They seemed to come out of my mouth before I had time to think about what I was saying. "We better be getting back to the group before Sir Gael catches us slacking off."

Suddenly the laughter came again. Talia's head snapped to the branches above us. She had heard the laughter too then.

"So you weren't really following *me*, were you?"

"I have no idea what you mean. I came to see if you were okay. That is all."

"Then you're saying you didn't hear that laughter?"

"What laughter?"

The laughter rang out as if in answer. When Talia's head snapped back up, I knew she had been lying, and she knew that I knew.

We stared at each other in a moment of pride and defiance. Finally, her eyes softened and her body relaxed. "Fine. Yes, I heard it. It makes me uneasy."

"What do you think is causing it? It sounds kind of beastly, doesn't it?"

"It is unlike anything I have ever heard before." Her body shuddered.

My curiosity as to what it might be was far greater than my fear of it. We needed to see what it was. My gaze landed on Talia's translucent wings. "Do you think you could fly up and get a better look?"

She was shifting her weight back and forth, fidgeting

with a necklace I hadn't noticed she wore around her neck. "I . . . I . . . I cannot do what you ask of me."

"What do you mean you can't?"

"I cannot fly. I never learned how, and now the muscles of my wings are not strong enough to carry me."

"You're a Fairy and yet you never learned how to fly?" This was unheard of.

"No." Her cheeks were growing red. I couldn't tell if it was from embarrassment or anger. Her eyes were focused on something on the ground.

"Why don't you fly?"

She glanced up at me, tears brimming her eyes. "My parents kept me grounded. I do not know why. They would say things like 'It is for your own good' and 'You will thank us later.' I have never understood it. I spent my life questioning their reasoning, but never got any answers. I tried to find other Fairies who would teach me, and I tried on my own too, but . . ." She turned her head away, wiping viciously at the water now flowing freely from her eyes. "Whenever my parents learned of it, they would clip my wings. The pain would keep me bedridden for weeks. I finally gave up."

"I'm sorry, Talia." I remembered the way she walked away when I asked her how she learned to fight, and Julio telling me about the deep desire to avenge her family. "How could you still care so strongly about what happened to them after all they did to you?"

"Because they are my parents. And despite all the pain they may have caused me, I could see the pain it was causing them too. They did not want to hurt me the way they did, and yet for some reason they truly felt it would be best for me. They loved me dearly, Zalan, and I will do everything I can to get their souls back from Belial."

I wanted to question her more, but the sound of laughter grew closer. This time it sounded like a snarl. A growl soon erupted, and something caused the branches to move. Something was coming toward us.

"Run!" I shouted.

Talia and I turned to do just that, but to our dismay, we watched as the branches of the tree began to extend toward the ground in front of us.

"That is impossible." Talia's eyes were round spheres of shock.

We were now surrounded by a wall of foliage. Trapped within the cocoon of the tree.

CHAPTER TEN

The Beast

"WHAT IS HAPPENING?" Talia's voice was higher than normal.

"Maybe it's simply the trees continual growth?"

"Continual growth?"

"Did you not notice how the bark on the tree keeps moving? This tree is growing at an exponential speed."

"I hope that is all this is." Talia moved closer to the green wall and drew her sword. She began hacking at the branches, to no avail. They simply grew right back as soon she cut through them.

"What if we tried climbing our way out?" I was already walking to the base of the tree. Just as I reached out to grab one of the lower hanging branches, I was flung to the side by something dark and moving quickly. I felt as if I had been hit by a boulder the size of Shilla.

A monster so large that it didn't make any sense why we couldn't see it before stood over me. The Minotaur had impressive horns, horns that could pack a punch with more strength than Commander Briggen. He snarled, saliva pooling from his mouth.

I could feel the branches behind me tear at the flesh of my back. A groan escaped my lips. I was sure there would be scars. My gut throbbed from the pain. My ribs reminded me I had already injured them in my earlier fall from the rope. My vision once more blurred from the pain.

The beast trained its attention on Talia. She had just

enough time to dodge his attack and pull her sword.

"Zalan?" Talia glanced at me, causing her to almost miss a blow from the beast. She charged the creature, sword aimed right for his chest. He stepped to the side at the last second, avoiding the blade.

"I'm fine. Just keep him at bay until I can get to my feet and help." I groaned, finding it hard to get the words out. I could do nothing but sit there and watch her fight. I had never felt so useless. I took a few staggering breaths before standing. I was going to fight one way or another.

I felt as if I would be sick, but pushing the bile back down, I drew my sword, thankful I'd had the frame of mind to grab it after the earlier fight. Gripping it as tightly as I could I attacked the Minotaur from behind. My weapon did not even break his skin. I took a step back, avoiding the Minotaur's horns as he spun to face me.

He snarled and growled in my face. The smell of rotting flesh hit me harder than his earlier attack had. I couldn't help but almost lose the contents of my stomach, again.

Talia made another attack with her sword, catching him in his side. The sword went deep enough that the beast should have been rendered motionless and blood should have been pouring from the wound. Neither of those things occurred. Instead, the beast yanked the sword from his side and flung it, along with Talia, into the trunk of the tree. She slumped to the ground and didn't move. I couldn't see if the impact had killed her. I surely hopped it hadn't. I wasn't strong enough to fight this beast. Without Talia's skilled attacks I was going to die.

"I saw what you did to those Pixies. I thought you would be more fun to fight."

I was shocked to hear the Minotaur speak. They were born and raised as animals, learning to growl and snarl, hunt, and attack. It was rare for one to know how to talk, let alone form whole sentences. I had to keep him talking. Maybe if I distracted him long enough, Talia would have the chance to come to.

"So you were the one we heard laughing then?"

"Maybe I was, maybe I wasn't."

"What was so funny?"

"I haven't had visitors in such a long time. I guess I was just giddy with joy."

His growl made the hairs on the back of my neck stand up.

Come on, Talia. I need you.

"This meadow has a way of pulling people in. I always found that strange, seeing as I'm here to keep people out. I guess it was a gift from the creator of this place. He must not want me getting too lonely."

"Creator? Who?"

"I'm not allowed to speak his name. It's one of the rules. Enough talking. I've not eaten in millennia and I am quite ravenous." He barred his teeth in a lip-curling smile.

This time I was ready for his charge and managed to dodge him just in time. He rammed into the wall and snarled. I had extended my arm just as he went passed me. My sword should have sliced through his arm, but there was no evidence that it had.

"Impossible."

"Ha, you stupid human, your weapons are useless against me."

He once more bent his head and ran straight for me. I wasn't able to dodge his move completely. His claw sliced through my leg. I crumpled to the ground, a scream exploding from my lungs.

The beast laughed, my blood dripping from his hand. He licked the blood. "Delicious. I can't wait to eat the rest of you."

I was definitely going to be sick.

This is it. This is where I die. First day on the quest and I will have already been slaughtered. Elyon, I know You and I have had our differences, but please, don't let me die before I can bring my father back home.

A memory floated to the surface of my mind. My father was leaving for the war. Mother was crying and hanging on to him, begging him not to go. I was pulling at his leg, my vision blurred from the tears.

He bent down to me, still holding my mother, and looked at both of us. He whispered something in her ear, then turned back to me, saying, "The future may be scary and uncertain, and sometimes we must face things we don't think we have the strength for, but, son, remember this: with Elyon all things are possible, and it is He who gives us strength so we can overcome all things."

Paladin had said it would take more than just my strength to get through this. He was right. I couldn't do it on my own. I needed more strength than I could possibly have. But I couldn't ask Elyon for help. I wouldn't. Not after all He had made me go through. For Mythica's sake, He was the one that put me in this position in the first place. No, I would find a way to defeat the beast on my own.

I managed to get to my knees, trying to find the strength to rise to my feet. I collapsed back down before I could even raise my sword.

No, I won't give in. I won't ask that monster for help.

I wedged my arms underneath me. Gritting my teeth against the pain of pushing myself back up. The Minotaur was laughing at me. Taunting me. I managed to stand, but as soon as I went to take another step, I crumbled.

Tears filled my eyes. The pain coursing through me was so severe, I felt as if I had been set on fire by Shilla herself. I wanted to die. I closed my eyes to do just that.

Images of running into my father's harms and embracing my sister once more appeared behind my eyes. Their smiles were beaming and tears were in their eyes, mirroring my own. I was happier than I had been in a very long time. But then my mother's tear-streaked face replaced those of my father and sister, although Mother's tears were of sadness not joy. She wept for my death. Shilla came and joined her, followed by the twins. They all mourned for me. I could feel their hearts breaking at the loss of my life.

I couldn't bear to look at them any longer. I couldn't bear the thought of them going through all that pain when I could have done something to prevent it.

Elyon, please don't let me die here. Don't let my mother have to mourn yet another loss. Forgive me for shutting You out. Please lend me Your strength to get through this, for I cannot do it without You.

A warmth spread across my body. I snapped my eyes open to see the Minotaur was looking at me, a puzzled expression on his gnarled face. His eyes widened in fear as I stood to my feet, no longer feeling the pain in my leg.

"It can't be. He said you didn't follow Elyon, that you wouldn't have His strength to help you."

"Throw your dagger. It will land its mark this time. You have My word."

I pulled my dagger once more from my boot. I reached back my arm and aiming for the beast's heart, I let my dagger fly. True to Elyon's word, the dagger penetrated the Minotaur's skin. The beast fell to the ground and laid motionless, his eyes still round circles of fear.

I starred at the dagger pierced through the chest of the beast. It was hard for me to believe it had really worked. That Elyon had actually answered my plea.

Thank You, Elyon.

All those years of hating Him still weighed on my

shoulders. I wasn't sure if I was ready to admit that I had been wrong, but maybe it was time to start considering that I was. Maybe Elyon wasn't the monster I had made Him to be, just maybe.

I ran to Talia to see if she was still breathing. Kneeling down next to her, I felt for a pulse. I let out a huge breath of air when I felt her heartbeat.

Talia began to stir at my touch. She slowly blinked her eyes open.

"Here, let me help you." I gently pulled her up into a sitting position. She looked around the clearing not saying a word, her eyes finally resting on the fallen beast. "Are you okay?"

Without moving her eyes, she answered, "Yeah, I think I am. How did you do it?"

"With Elyon's strength."

She turned to me, a smile on her face.

"That's the first time I have heard you speak positively of Him." I shrugged. "Why do you suppose he attacked?" She gestured toward the Minotaur.

"He seemed to be protecting the tree. Although I don't know why. The tree seems pretty capable of protecting itself."

"I wonder . . ." She looked around the clearing. "What if he wasn't protected the tree but working with it? What if they *both* were protecting something?"

Talia moved to the base of the tree and began pocking around the roots. The tree moved in response.

The ground beneath us began to shake. We fell hard as the roots of the tree came up from the ground and slithered toward us, wrapping around our ankles before we had the chance to get out from their reach. Talia once more readied her sword and quickly began slicing at the roots, but they grew right back. My dagger wasn't going to be nearly as efficient as her sword, but I started hacking at them anyway.

We finally managed to free our legs and get back on our feet.

More roots had begun to pull up from the ground and were reaching toward us. Talia and I slashed at them with everything we had. Talia had begun to swing her sword in a circle, creating a fan of protection. I glanced behind us to see if I could find a weak point in the wall of roots, only to find they had burrowed their way underneath us and were starting to attack from behind. I moved so my back was to Talia's.

It felt like we weren't making any progress. Whatever injuries we caused quickly healed. We were engaged in a battle I didn't think we could win.

Elyon, why did You help me out of one peril, only to let me face another? My anger and hatred quickly rekindled. I questioned why I ever let myself believe that Elyon would want to do anything but watch me suffer.

In between strikes I tried to figure out the best way to stop the tree. It had to have a weak spot; it was just a matter of finding it. That's when I noticed a group of roots pulling close to one particular area of the tree, near the base of the trunk. They wouldn't stretch out as far as the others. Were they trying to protect a vulnerable part of the tree? That had to be the way to end the fight. If it wasn't, we were surely dead.

"Talia, I have an idea. Try and keep the tree's attention on you and away from me," I shouted over my shoulder. Talia nodded, too focused on her attacks to offer more.

I took a few steps back, trying to see if I could see an opening in the roots by the base of the tree. The tree appeared to realize I was no longer close and slowed its advances toward me, instead sending more of its roots to fight Talia, who looked as if she was about to run out of steam.

I waited a moment longer, calculating the timing and making sure I would be able to hit the right spot. Finally, an opening appeared. I took the opportunity and drove my dagger right into the trunk of the tree, just barely missing being sideswiped by a root. The root fell limp before it had a chance to hit me. A loud cracking noise came next, much like wood being splintered, before all of the limbs collapsed, lifeless. The trees began to whither and fall. Talia and I jumped out of the way, only to trip in the piles of roots at our feet. I threw my arms over my head. I could feel branches begin to hit us. Suddenly there was a loud thud, and the ground shook. I didn't dare move.

"Zalan?" Talia's voice was close. I lowered my arms and peered over to where she lay next to me. Through the branches that surrounded us, I could see there was a smile on her face. "We did it."

I reached my hand to move the branches on top of me, and they crumpled to dust in my hands. I began to push at more branches and they disintegrated as well. Soon Talia was doing the same, until we were both free from the tree's grasp and covered in dust.

We made our way to the base of the tree. It no longer hummed or glowed. The life and magic in the tree were gone.

I went to retrieve my dagger and saw something peeking out of the dust-covered ground. I bent down and dug out the object. It was an old leather box no bigger than Kitsune's paw. As I brushed off the dust, I yelled over to Talia, "I think I found whatever it was trying to protect."

Talia quickly came over to where I was standing and peered down at the box. I was looking at the picture of a set of armor woven in gold thread on the top when she grabbed it from my hands. Talia gingerly opened the top.

"We found it, Zalan. We found the Belt of Truth."

CHAPTER ELEVEN

The Belt

I COULDN'T BELIEVE IT. Not only had I actually allowed Elyon in, but He had responded and He had led us to the first piece of Armor. I never imagined we would find it as quickly as we did. I also didn't realize how hard it would be. My ribs hurt and breathing was difficult. I felt as if I was about to pass out. If this was only one of many battles to come, I wasn't sure I wanted to continue.

"Let's get it back to the others. Maybe Sir Gael will be so pleased with our finding the Belt that he'll stop pushing me so hard."

Talia laughed, harder than I thought the joke deserved, but the sound made my heart break. It made me extremely happy to hear her laughter. Memories of her scream came rushing in. All remnants of joy was gone. "Sir Gael does not seem like someone to go easy on you. He has been pushing you harder than the rest of us. Why?"

I had been so taken aback by the sound of her screams in my head that I had almost forgotten about the Armor and Sir Gael.

"What?" I mumbled, still trying to shake off the feeling of dread.

"You and Sir Gael seem to have a rivalry going."

"Oh, yeah, we have a unique relationship. I may or may not have disregarded his standing when we first met. I don't think he has forgiven me, but I do know he is challenging me to be a better person. Isn't forgiveness a requirement as a follower of Elyon?"

Her smile disappeared. She gently closed the box and began walking toward the tree's wall. This time when she pulled her sword across the branches, they crumbled.

I was beginning to wonder if she would ever answer, but when the last of the branches fell, she did.

"Yes, but it does not mean it is an easy task, and some of us take longer to reach the point where we can finally let go." She got quiet, obviously thinking about her own desire of revenge and the forgiveness she has not yet granted those who took her family from her.

We continued walking in silence. The meadow was no longer filled with that strange feeling. The wind and plants were behaving as if nothing had happened. This time when I walked through the tall plants, I trampled them under my feet.

Once we reached the tree lining, we both looked back and gasped. The tree that had just fought us was completely gone. There was no evidence of it ever being there. If it were not for the box Talia held, I would have thought the whole thing was in my imagination.

The walk felt longer than it had before. I wasn't sure if it was because I was fatigued from the fight or if it had something to do with the strange magic around the tree.

When we arrived back, the others were still interrogating the Pixies. None of them seemed to have noticed we had left. Talia and I looked at each other for a moment in confusion. Surely at least Sir Gael would have noted our absence.

"Guys, there is no more need to question the Pixies. We found it."

Everyone looked up, probably surprised to see us with bruises and cuts we didn't have before.

"What happened to you guys? You both look like you

have been used for a practice dummy." Kitsune was sitting up on her back haunches, her head tilted to the side in curiosity.

"We were in that meadow." Talia gestured in the general direction of where we had come from.

"You two look like you have been in quite the tussle. How did you manage to get so banged up so quickly? We just finished our fight with the Pixies moments ago."

"What do you mean? We've been gone for quite some time."

Some of the Pixies began to rise and inch away. No one took notice or cared.

Talia and I looked at each other. There must have been something in the magic of the meadow that had manipulated time. What had been long to us had only been minutes to the rest of the group.

Sage finally asked, "What is it that you found?" Her eyes were ablaze with hope and curiosity, yet her stance was one of indifference.

Talia pulled the box from under her arm and opened it so the others could see what was inside. The symphony of gasps that followed brought a smile to my lips. A sudden sting caused me to wipe my tongue across my mouth. This cut would take some time to heal. I wondered how many other injuries I would discover across my body.

"There is one more thing. Sir Gael, the beast we encountered protecting this was a Shadow." Talia's voice held much more than a hint of fear.

Sir Gael seemed to come out of a daze. "Are you sure? If it really is, then we have more problems than originally thought. Shadows take powerful magic to create, and if Belial is using them to guard the Armor, then he's gained more power than Paladin knows. You're certain it was indeed a Shadow?"

Talia stood up straighter, her eyes showing her anger that

he would question her. "I am sure. There was no mistaking the smell of rotting flesh, and when we cut him, there was no blood."

"We need to inform Paladin of this right away. Julio, you are the fastest. We have not gone too far from the palace. You will take a written letter directly to Paladin himself. We will reconnect with you at the Valley of the Lost."

"Sir Gael, with all due respect, that will leave you down a man, and I am the strongest here."

"I have faith that Elyon will protect us. There will be no further questioning my decision. I just need a moment to compose the letter."

We headed back out of the forest to where we had had left our horses and Sir Gael sat down and wrote the letter. I watched Julio as he stormed across the small campsite, making sure all his supplies were secure. He didn't appear pleased at all to find himself going back to the palace so soon.

It seemed odd that he would get so upset about leaving us for just a day's time. With his speed he would be able to quickly catch back up to us. I was thinking about speaking to him when fatigue from the day's battles caught up with me and I went to lie down on my mat before Sir Gael had a chance to bark another order.

Sir Gael looked up from writing and frowned, then turned his gaze to Talia and did the same.

"You two are in no condition to continue on. Sage, tend to their injuries the best you can."

Sage stood up from where she was rolling out her mat, a look of disgust on her face. She dug through her pack and pulled out a box before trotting over to us.

"You don't have to help us if you don't want to."

She looked as if she had been caught doing something she shouldn't. "Forgive me. I have little desire to be around blood. It makes me queasy. I only learned how to tend wounds out of necessity for the war. Many of my people come back with injuries that were never treated."

Talia took Sage's hand in hers. "Please, let us tend to ourselves. It will be good practice for us both."

Sage looked relieved and placed the box in Talia's hands before going back to her mat.

Talia opened the box and pulled out a small tube. She read the label, then smeared the contents across my lip. Her touch sent a shiver down my body, a reaction that caused her to laugh.

"Did I forget to mention it would sting a little?"

I laughed too, not having even noticed the stinging.

"I need to take a look at your ribs. I can tell you are having a tough time breathing." She motioned for me to remove my shirt, her cheeks reddening slightly.

I did as she requested, but the pain caused me to wince.

After looking at my bare chest for a moment she handed me the bandage from the box. "You will need to wrap these around your chest tightly. The bruising does not look too severe, and your ribs should heal nicely."

She moved to work on my other scrapes as I began to wrap my abdomen. Once I was finished I attempted to put my shirt back on but found it difficult. I decided I would go without, causing Talia to redden even more. She handed over the tube of ointment, and I began to gently wipe at her scrapes as she had mine.

Trying to ease the awkward silence between us I asked her, "What's a Shadow? I've never heard of them before."

"You are lucky. Where I come from, they are all too common. A Shadow is a monster. They are creatures of Belial's making."

"I thought Belial was incapable of creating life."

"He is. The Shadows are not living. That is what is so dangerous about them. Shadows are the bodies of Elyon's creations. Belial takes control of their anatomy after they have died and fills them with his evil spirits. The soul of the Minotaur we fought today had long since left and been replaced by a demon."

"How could Elyon allow such creatures to exist?"

"Well, Zalan, that is not an easy question to answer; however, I will try. Elyon created everyone with their own free will. That includes Belial. That is why good and evil both exist. Elyon chooses not to control Belial's will, although He does care enough about us that He will protect us against those forces and will intervene when needed. He will not stop Belial from creating the Shadows, but He will eventually regain control and destroy them. He is the creator of their bodies and the ruler of the spiritual realm, after all."

I sat there in silence contemplating what she said. It seemed strange to me that a God so loving and caring could allow so much evil to exist. However, Talia had a point. Elyon created us with the ability to make our own choices. If He destroyed all evil in Mythica, we would lose our ability to choose.

Elyon, forgive me for ever doubting Your goodness. I'm learning more and more about who You truly are. Thank You for Your patience with me.

I could feel a warmth spread throughout my body. I could feel the love Elyon had for me despite the hatred I held toward Him for years.

With our wounds patched up as best we could, we curled on our mats and slept. At least I tried to. My mind kept replaying the events of the last couple of days. So much had happened. There was a tingling in the air I couldn't place my finger on. It seemed charged with tense energy, but everyone had long since fallen asleep.

My eyes were finally becoming heavy when a loud thud came from within the camp. I looked around to see what had made the sound. No one else seemed to have heard it. An uneasiness began to creep over me. Forgetting my injured ribs, I tried to get up. At their reminder, I moved a little more gingerly.

I walked slowly around the perimeter of the camp, trying to make as little noise as possible. When I didn't see anything out of the ordinary, I made my way back toward my mat. That's when I noticed it. The box that contained the Belt of Truth had fallen out of Sir Gael's satchel. I chastised myself for being so jumpy and went to put the box back.

As soon as my hand touched the box, I pulled back. The box was warm. I carefully reached for the box once more and slowly opened the lid; a soft light was glowing within.

That's odd. It wasn't glowing before. I opened the lid the rest of the way to see what might be causing the light. It seemed to be coming from the Belt itself. I hadn't gotten a close look at the Belt before, and now that I had, it took my breath away. Much like the palace, it was simple yet had an air of elegance. Words had been carved into the design of the Belt, written in the old tongue. My hand reached for it before I even had time to register what I was doing.

"Do not touch that." Sir Gael's voice come suddenly from behind. I spun around in surprise. Sir Gael's eyes were wild with anger. "Fool, do you not remember Paladin's warning. Anyone who is not the warrior will be burned."

"I . . . I . . . I . . . wasn't thinking."

Sir Gael seemed calm. "No harm done, I guess. Just hand over the box before you do something stupid."

My cheeks flared at his jab. I was closing the box when my hand accidently brushed the Belt. I sucked in a puff of air.

I glanced up at Sir Gael to see his eyes had narrowed. "Is everything all right?" he spat out. "Just hand over the box. Now." His lips were in a thin, tight line.

"Sir Gael, I brushed the Belt and didn't burn." Instead,

there was been a pleasant heat.

"You did what?" he bellowed, his eyes taking on that wild look I had seen just moments before. "It cannot be. Impossible."

"It's true. See." I moved to pull the Belt from the box.

No sooner had my hand touched the Belt then Sir Gael let out an ear-piercing scream and lunged for the box, but it was too late. I already grasped the Belt in my hand. I knew the truth. My gut dropped from the sudden knowledge, the betrayal. I had been so stupid, so blind.

"Zalan, listen to me." Sir Gael moved to grab my arm but I pulled back.

"No, I'll never listen to you. It was you all along, all this time working right alongside Paladin."

I was dizzy with the revelation.

"Yes, it was me. Belial will be pleased to know that he was right. That it was you who were destined."

Hearing him admit to his treachery made me sick to my stomach. I felt like I would pass out.

I looked down at the Belt of Truth and was startled to see that I could now read the inscription: "Stand strong and fasten Truth around your waist like a belt." Truth had been granted to me, and Truth was what I saw. Truth was what would destroy me.

I felt the darkness that I had been evading for so long suddenly overtake me. One last thought flickered through my mind before I was consumed by the nothingness.

Sir Gael was the spy, and I indeed was the Warrior.

ACKNOWLEDGMENTS

First and foremost, all credit ultimately goes to Elyon Himself. He was the one to place the dream of becoming a writer into my heart, and without His imagination and guidance, I never would have made it this far.

To my brothers and sisters for walking beside me in this process and for always rooting for me, thank you doesn't begin to describe it.

For my dad for always being my first editor and reader, I love you more than infinity.

And many thanks to Self-Publishing school and everyone involved for pushing me to get my book out there at last.

Self-Publishing
School

NOW IT'S YOUR TURN

**Discover the EXACT 3-step blueprint you need
to become a bestselling author in as little as 3 months.**

Self-Publishing School helped me, and now I want them to help you with this FREE resource to begin outlining your book!

Even if you're busy, bad at writing, or don't know where to start, you CAN write a bestseller and build your best life.

With tools and experience across a variety of niches and professions, Self-Publishing School is the only resource you need to take your book to the finish line!

DON'T WAIT

Say "YES" to becoming a bestseller:

https://self-publishingschool.com/friend/

Follow the steps on the page to get a FREE resource to get started on your book and unlock a discount to get started with Self-Publishing School.